BILLIONAIRE FOR NEW YEAR'S

Billionaire For New Year's

Em Brown

ISBN: 978-1-63161-026-4

Published by TCK Publishing
www.TCKPublishing.com

CONTENTS

1

She's going *where?*" Rance Durand asked with a shake of his head after the squash ball ricocheted off his temple. He couldn't have heard his friend correctly.

"Trey's Naughty Noel party," Blaine repeated. "He hosts it every year before Christmas. I'm telling you: you should go, Durand."

So he hadn't heard wrong. Rance retrieved the ball from the corner of the court. He still couldn't believe it. "Audrey and Trey know each other?"

"Charlene knows Trey."

Charlene was Audrey's best friend. It didn't surprise him that Charlene would know someone like Trey Harriman, whose family wealth afforded him a life of leisure, which Trey filled with all manner of sexual escapades. His level of sexual activity dwarfed even

Blaine's, and Blaine could average a different woman every week.

Blaine presented his hand, but Rance held onto the ball aimlessly. He pressed his lips into a firm line before saying, "That doesn't mean Audrey is going to the party."

"You mean you don't *want* her to go to the party," Blaine translated.

"I mean it's too raunchy for her tastes. I don't think she does parties involving sexual debauchery with strangers."

Even as he said it, Rance had to remind himself that Audrey Jones had once elected to call an escort service. That was how they had met two years ago, right before Christmas. He had impersonated her date from the service and gotten her to fall in love with him over the course of seven unforgettable days. That was followed by what was the happiest year of his life. The thought of marriage had cropped up several times in his mind.

A wistful pang rose in his chest. It had been months since they had broken up, but he still missed her. At times he found it hard to believe that they were no longer together.

"Dude, you sound like a prude," Blaine responded. "Even my great-grandmother sounds more exciting."

Rance opened his mouth to object. It had been his own idea to impersonate a gigolo with Audrey. Granted, he'd never done anything like that in his life before, but he'd played his part convincingly. He'd relished all the different things he could do to her body. All the different ways he could make her come. No doubt Blaine considered himself a sexual demi-god, but Rance was sure he could give his friend a good run.

"Don't guys stop using the word 'dude' in high school?" Rance said instead.

"It's a Southern California thing. You foreigners wouldn't understand. You gonna hand over the ball or what?"

Blaine liked to mock Rance's French heritage even though Rance had been living in the United States since starting college at Stanford over fifteen years ago. He threw Blaine the ball, and to show his college roommate what 'foreigners' could do, Rance returned the serve extra hard. They exchanged volleys until Rance whipped the ball into the corner and had the satisfaction of watching Blaine crash into the wall in a failed effort to get to the ball.

"Nice shot," Blaine complimented with a rattle of his head. Beads of sweat fell from his sandy blond hair. He jogged back to his side of the court. "So you gonna go?"

"To Trey's party? Why? Because Audrey might go?"

The prospect of Audrey attending did perk his interest. Or rather, a possessive jealousy. On the one hand, he didn't think he could stand watching someone try to pick up on her. On the other, staying at home imagining the worst wasn't any better. But it wasn't any of his business what Audrey did or didn't do. They weren't together anymore.

"Because *I'm* going."

"Don't tell me you need a date," Rance said wryly.

"Hell no. Not that you're not a good-looking guy, Durand. I'm sure you'd make a good catch in the Castro."

Rance didn't need Blaine's assurances. While his body wasn't as muscular or as evenly tanned as Blaine's, it was lean and toned. Women liked the way a pair of jeans fitted over his long legs and hard ass. After getting over her initial disappointment that he looked more like Colin Firth than Denzel Washington, Audrey had found enjoyment in running her fingers over his pecs and through the loose curls of his hair. She had been fascinated with the softness of his hair. And something in the way her fingers moved over his head, gently scraping his scalp, never failed to send provocative prickles to his groin.

"I bat for just one team," continued Blaine. "My problem is I can't decide whether I should take Julia or Angela to the Naughty Noel."

"I'm surprised you're not taking both."

"Yeah. I already proposed a threesome with Angela. She didn't go for it. Maybe I should go stag. Trey always has hotties at his parties. Another reason you should go."

"I don't think Stephanie would go for that," Rance said as he served the ball again.

"Stephanie's a hottie. I'll give you that. But you two haven't been dating that long." Blaine returned the serve.

"And if she finds out I went to Trey's Naughty Noel, there won't be any future dates."

"Yeah, she's a bit stuffy. Audrey was more fun."

Rance backhanded the ball without a word. Even if he agreed with Blaine, there was no sense in making comparisons.

"If you get hit with another case of jungle fever, you should go for Charlene. Talk about *hot* chocolate..."

Charlene had a near perfect body, tall and slender, with perky breasts and long legs extending from what Blaine called 'bodacious buttocks.' But Rance liked the curves that Audrey had. Audrey had substance. She was voluptuous. Succulent. He loved the way her delicious thighs wrapped around him, the way her breasts weighed heavily in his hands, the feel of her ass against his groin when he took her from behind.

He also loved the glow in her eyes when she looked at him after they had made love. Loved the conversations they had before, during, and after. He loved her bluntness, her fearless questions about anything and everything, her self-deprecating humor, and the moments when she revealed her vulnerability. Most of all, he loved the way he felt when he was with her.

"I'm surprised you haven't hit on Charlene yet," Rance remarked as he dribbled the ball atop his racket. They had played for a solid hour, but he was too distracted by thoughts of Audrey to want to play another set.

"I have," Blaine replied. "She turned me down. Playing hard to get. You know how women are. I should try again at the party. So you goin' or what?"

Rance bounced the little black ball and served it perfectly against the opposite wall. As much as he would have liked to see Audrey, going to Trey's party served no purpose at all.

"You're on your own," he told Blaine.

"I ain't dating a white guy again," Charlene said as she and Audrey watched Blaine and Trey bump chests across the dimly lit, crowded living room of Trey's home. Wall sconces and a throbbing red strobe light provided the only illumination. All the furniture had been cleared from the room except for a few sofas and end tables lining the walls and two dancing cages, decorated with tinsel and occupied by scantily dressed women, standing on either side of the DJ and his table. Erotic photos of nudes lined the walls. Mistletoe hung from the vaulted ceilings. And instead of bowls of potpourri, there were bowls of condoms everywhere.

Anticipation briefly crept up Audrey's throat. Since Blaine was here, was it possible that Rance might also be here? She hadn't seen Rance in months. The last she had heard he was seeing a Pacific Heights socialite. She'd seen the woman's picture in a recent edition of the *Nob Hill Gazette*. Stephanie was a gorgeous blonde with golden highlights in her hair. She could have been in one of those Pantene shampoo commercials. She had perfect make-up, of course, so she could also have been in a L'Oréal ad. Measurements were probably 36-26-30. A far cry from Audrey's measurements.

"I don't know why I let you talk me into coming here," Audrey said after it was clear that Blaine had arrived by himself. Disappointment replaced the anticipation.

"So you could show off that new dress of yours. Admit it, you weren't going to get much use out of it otherwise. You wouldn't want to blow the four hundred bucks you spent on it."

Audrey glanced down at her gold sheath with black satin trim before narrowing her eyes at Charlene. "*You* convinced me to buy the dress."

"Because you look smokin' in it."

"True."

She had not needed much convincing from Charlene. Truth was she had wanted to reward herself for having stuck to her latest diet and fitness routine. The benefit of not being in a relationship was that she had a lot of extra time to work out. Actually, since breaking up with Rance, she had initially reverted back to her old ways, finding comfort with two other men: Ben and Jerry. And when they weren't available, there was Häagen-Dazs and the occasional Breyer's.

She had also filled up the lonely hours with work and even found herself doing the filing that belonged to her assistant at Stevenson & Young, where she was now a senior vice-president. But working was what had contributed to the end of her relationship. It had served as a convenient excuse not to attend social functions with Rance. Although Blaine and Alan, his two best friends from Stanford, had always made her feel welcome, she didn't fit in his world. He hadn't seemed different from her at first, but it turned out they were vastly different worlds—and not just because he was half English, half French while she was born and raised in the flats of Richmond, California. Rance's family founded DHRG, the Durand Hotel and Restaurant Group, which, after a few mergers and acquisitions, now encompassed over 150 luxury boutique hotels and restaurants in over 100 cities worldwide. . She was the daughter of a social worker and a custodian. She would have never thought she could spend four hundred dollars on a single clothing item. Growing up in North Richmond, a splurge meant buying something from the fifty-percent-off rack at Macy's. And clothes that came off that rack were usually out of season. You couldn't wear whatever you bought until next year.

"You don't understand," she remembered saying to Rance. "A black woman just has to work harder to get ahead."

She remembered how he had pressed his lips into a firm line—a clear signal that he was angry. He had nice lips. Usually the lips on a white man were indiscernible to her, but his made her salivate. And they felt divine on her body.

"Don't play the race card," Rance had replied. "You know damn well I don't question that fact. But you still have a choice, Audrey. A *personal* choice. You're choosing work."

And not me, was the unsaid summary. Only she didn't realize that at the time. She knew she had felt guilty and knew, deep down, that Rance was right. But she hadn't wanted to admit it at the time. So she had turned her guilt into indignation. How dare he try to criticize her priorities? Sure, he had reduced the amount of traveling his work required so that he could stay in San Francisco more, but it was easier for a white male to rearrange his work life. If she had tried to do the same, she ran the risk of being viewed as lazy, of not wanting her advancement bad enough.

And then she had accused him of not supporting her. Granted, she had turned down a huge opportunity in her company's Philadelphia office shortly after meeting Rance and decided that she wasn't going to make her life about her career. But her latest promotion was still a big deal, and she wasn't going to reward her company by slacking off. What if things didn't work out between her and Rance? She would have denied her career advancement for nothing.

Charlene interrupted her reverie. "Oooh, girl, that brother is checking you out."

Audrey looked through the crowd and thought she made out a man in a cream sweater and beige slacks. "It's too hard to tell if he's looking at me. It's dark in here."

"Of course he's looking at you. You're the second hottest looking sister in here."

Charlene flashed an impish smile. Audrey wouldn't have argued with her. Charlene was blessed with a great body and the ability to consume all the chocolate she wanted without adding an inch to her waistline.

But this time Audrey was too pleased with how she looked in her own short hip-hugger to dwell on such injustices. She had gone down one full dress size. A damn good accomplishment given that six weeks ago she couldn't fit into her clothes, including her tummy control underwear. That was when she had emptied her freezer of Rocky Road, Chocolate Chip Cookie Dough and the obligatory low fat Cherry Garcia frozen yogurt. Instead of going into the office on Saturdays, she went to the gym. Work didn't seem to mean as much anyway without Rance. Strange how that was.

"How would you like to make it with him in a dark room?" Charlene asked. "Trey told me that there are eight bedrooms upstairs and they are all *open to the public.*"

"Pass," Audrey said.

"At least be open to the idea. What'd you come here for if you didn't want to have a little fun?"

"Honestly? I didn't want to be home alone on a Saturday night watching reruns of *Deal or No Deal* on the Game Show Network."

"I'll make it worth your while. I'll hook you up with a serious hottie."

But an hour later Charlene was busy gyrating hips with a guy that resembled a young Russell Wong. Which was fine with Audrey. The only thing she knew for sure she was getting friendly with was the eggnog. Everywhere she looked she saw couples getting hot and heavy: men with women, women with women, and men with men. And it went past the dirty dancing, wet kissing, or passionate groping that one might find in a party full of over-hormonal teenagers. Some couples might as well have been making a live porno. Audrey witnessed one man shimmy the jeans off another. When she got a full view of his lumpy white ass, she decided to search out some fresh air and drink her eggnog in peace.

Avoiding the mistletoe, she made her way up the tinsel-decorated stairs to the top floor of the house. It would have the best view. She touched the handle of the door at the end of the hall and paused. Although Charlene had said that the entire house was open to the guests, Audrey wasn't used to exploring a stranger's house on her own. Plus, who knew what she would find behind closed doors? But she was a sucker for a good vista ever since Rance had shown her all the picture perfect spots in the city. Some of the best views were from the outside looking in, and Marin County offered some of the best in that respect.

She turned the handle and pushed open the door. Silence, not a raging orgy, greeted her. She stepped into the dark bedroom suite, lit only by a few votive candles on either side of a king-sized bed, and inhaled sharply at the view beyond the double glass doors on the wall opposite her. Charlene had said the house was easily worth several million, and Audrey suspected the view accounted for a good chunk of the house's value despite its large square footage and luxury rooms.

Two sliding glass doors on either side of the bed led to a balcony. She crossed the room and let herself out. A blast of the winter air made her skin prickle, so she went to stand beneath a heating lamp. The lights of the city and its two bridges twinkled like those of a Christmas tree. She loved the way the moonlight glanced off the waves of the bay. Situated between a bay and the ocean, San Francisco was the perfect combination of city and nature. She let out a sigh. What was it about views that made one sentimental? Was it because views were always associated with romance? Was it because beauty was meaningful when shared?

The sound of shuffling and grunting made her glance away from the million-dollar view and down to the deck below where a guy was getting it on with two women. He hoisted one of the women onto the wooden railing and began kissing her as if he hadn't eaten for days. The other woman nestled herself on her knees in front of him, unzipped his pants, and began massaging the bulge at his crotch. Audrey watched them with mild curiosity. She could never make out like that in such a public place.

Except with Rance. He had a way of making her forget where they were – or titillating her with the location. They had fucked in the men's locker room at the *Hotel sur Mer*, one of the hotels he owned and operated for his family. He had also bent her out a fourth story window and fucked her from behind. It had been late at night, but she had never done anything so brazen before. Her body temperature went up a notch remembering that someone had walked by below them.

The woman on her knees had freed the guy's cock and was sucking it vigorously. Meanwhile, the woman on the railing had pulled down the top of her dress and was pushing the guy's face into her breasts. Audrey wondered if she could ever share a guy with another woman. The picture of her, Rance, and one of the women below flashed before her. Surprisingly, she found the idea provocative. Not surprisingly, she would have also wanted to beat the other woman to a pulp.

Okay, so she couldn't share Rance. But how about a stranger? A guy with whom she would only engage in meaningless sex and never see again afterwards? Maybe. Or maybe it would be two guys instead of two women. Now that was a threesome she could get into. One of the guys could look like Taye Diggs. The other could look like…Rance Durand.

Shaking her head, Audrey looked away from the threesome and out at the redwoods framing the view. It was the holidays and she wasn't with anyone, so naturally she was fixated on her ex-boyfriends. Correction: one of her ex-boyfriends. She wasn't thinking about the cop she had dated before Rance or the arrogant Oreo from Wharton. Just Rance. She finished off the rest of her eggnog in one gulp.

She contemplated how much time she was going to have to spend on the stair climber to work off all the eggnog she had consumed. More than she thought, she concluded as she noticed the trees in front of her looked a bit blurry. Of course the eggnog had been spiked. She hadn't tasted the brandy at first through all the cinnamon and nutmeg. Leaning against the railing, she went back to looking at the threesome below. The man had his hand between the legs of the woman in front of him, but he was getting visibly distracted by what was being done to him by the other woman. The woman on the railing tried to refocus his attention by fondling her tits and pushing them up at his face. Audrey felt warmth spreading through her loins and shifted her weight. Well, damn, she was getting turned on. She wondered if she was going to be the only guest at the party not getting any.

"Which of the women would you rather be?" a husky voice behind her asked.

"Is that a trick question?" Audrey replied. She meant it as a glib retort but the throaty quality in which it came out sounded flirty instead.

"Sometimes it is more exciting to give pleasure than to receive it."

He was standing really close to her. She had no space to turn around, at least not without grazing most of her body against his, so she continued to lean against the railing. As if in response to what he had said, the two women below both began moaning.

"'Tis the season of giving, I suppose," she said. It wasn't the most witty response, but she wasn't sure what to do with the mystery intruder. She wasn't ready to encourage him. If he expected to receive a blowjob just because, he could forget about it. But something in the way he spoke gave her goosebumps.

"And what would you wish to receive?" He placed a hand on the railing near her.

His palpable heat seemed to touch her."An orgasm wouldn't be bad."

Shit. Did that come out of her mouth? Damn the eggnog.

"Is that all?"

Is that all? Was he criticizing her answer?

"Well," she drawled, "I could wish for world peace, too, but then I'd sound like a damn beauty pageant queen."

He chuckled.

"I'm a simple girl," she added.

"There are many ways to achieve an orgasm. Perhaps you prefer some to others?"

Despite the power of the heating lamp, she could sense his body heat hovering behind her. He had a fresh scent, rather like the pines and redwoods surrounding them. He ran a finger gently along her forearm and up to her bare shoulder. His finger trailed to the center of her upper back where her shoulder blades met. She shivered. Was she about to get it on with a complete stranger? Well, it wouldn't be the first time, given how she and Rance had met. And something in the way this man spoke was comforting.

He wasn't just a drunken idiot. Maybe she could just see how it would go for a little bit...

"I'm not picky," she replied.

2

Rance held his breath. He had been wrong. Trey's Naughty Noel wasn't too risqué for Audrey, though he wasn't surprised to have found her alone in a remote part of the house instead of engaging in the bumping and grinding downstairs. Her response had woken up every inch of his body as if icy water coursed through his veins, but he couldn't tell if he was excited or madly jealous that she hadn't rebuked him as he had half-expected her to do.

This was not at all what he had thought he would find himself doing. He had told Blaine he wasn't even coming. But the prospect of seeing Audrey was too much of a lure. He wanted to find out how she was doing. He had expected to engage in conversation with all the obligatory questions about work, family, and perhaps even the significant other. Through all that, he would be trying to detect whether or not she might have missed him.

But all that had changed when he saw how incredible she looked in her tight dress and heels. She had been working out. The observation made his cock stir with jealousy. She had never tried to look so hot while she had been dating him.

He massaged the shoulder that he had kissed, then the base of her neck, up the side to the area beneath her ear. She let out a soft groan. Stepping to her, he threaded his arms below her armpits and up past her chest, locking her in place against him. His hands circled around the back of her neck. He tried not to groan audibly as he felt her ass press against his groin.

"You must be a masseur," she murmured, melting against him as he massaged her neck.

"I'm in the business of providing people an enjoyable experience," he admitted.

"That can mean anything. You could be the neighborhood ice cream truck driver."

He smiled. "Do you like ice cream?"

"Honey, I'm all about the ice cream. Best invention ever."

"Better than sex?"

"Sex ain't an invention. But I would give the edge to ice cream these days."

Rance shook his head. What was it with women and dessert? It was one thing to compete against another man for a woman's affection, but starches and chocolate were not something he had been prepared for. And just when he thought he had conquered tiramisu, along came molten chocolate cake.

"I'd like to give the edge back to sex," he said, brushing his lips against the nape of her neck. He breathed in the scent of her perfume, a subtle musk, nothing too floral or sweet.

He dropped his hands to her hips. He loved the swell of a woman's hips, and Audrey would always have that full hourglass shape, no matter how much weight she lost.

"God, you are beautiful," he uttered, mostly to himself.

"I won't argue with you."

His cock throbbed. With a low growl, he began caressing her neck with his lips. She melted against him. He slid his hands down the fullness of her thighs and skimmed the bare flesh below the hem of her dress. She felt smooth and supple. Desire swirled inside him, heating his groin and making him dizzy . As much as he admired how sexy she looked in her dress, he wanted nothing more than to rip it off her body right now. Below their balcony, the man in the threesome gasped in climax.

"Stay as you are," Rance instructed in a low whisper.

Heart pounding, he untied the decorative red satin ribbon that was twined around the banister. He wrapped it around her eyes. She hadn't glanced his way so far, and he didn't know how she would react if she found out it was him. She might be pleasantly surprised or she might be angry and offended, leaving him no hope of recovering the past. He couldn't take that chance.

"What's this for?" she asked.

He heard her hesitation and answered, "To broaden the imagination."

He grabbed another ribbon and wrapped her wrists together.

"So you won't go anywhere," he explained as he bound her wrists to the railing.

She inhaled sharply.

"Do you hear the women below?"

They listened to the moaning and whimpering.

"I hope you'll be echoing their sentiments," he told her.

This time her breath indicated she was inclined. Lifting the hem of her dress, he parted her thighs and slid his fingers past the edge of her thong. She had trimmed, he noted. Possibly expecting to make it with someone. Of course she did. Why else would someone attend Trey's party? The surge of jealousy made his cock harden further. When he found her wet, he thought he'd go crazy.

Forcing himself to take a deep breath, he paced himself, gently swirling his fingers against her clitoris. She moaned her pleasure. He strummed the engorged nub with more vigor. She began panting. The wetness increased. Her head fell back against his chest. He breathed in the scent of her shampoo and gloried in the hot flesh surrounding his hand. Her breath quickened, matching the acceleration of the grunting and groaning below. Finding the spot that made her legs quiver, he rubbed her harder and faster, pushing her over the edge, making her cry out in pleasure. He let her down gently from her climax, slowing his rhythm and lightening his touch until the last of the waves racking her body had subsided.

That was as far as he had intended to take it, despite his raging hard-on. But he was filled with the smell of her, the look of her, the feel of her. The pulsating music from inside the house and the symphony of moans below seemed to wrap the two of them in an atmosphere of sexual arousal. He would have to leave Audrey and either escape the party altogether or find a private place to service himself.

"Oh, baby," Audrey exhaled. "That was as good as ice cream."

That did it. He bent her over the rail and unzipped his pants.

"Wh—" she began.

"Don't worry. I have a condom," he said.

Blaine had slipped him one, insisting that one couldn't go through the party without carrying some rubber.

With one hand he massaged her through her now sopping thong. With the other, he held the condom packet and tore it open using his teeth. He rolled it down his shaft. His breath became ragged at the thought of what he was about to do. He was going to fuck his ex-girlfriend without her knowing who he was. And she was apparently okay getting fucked by a perfect stranger. Suppressing the desire to ram his cock without ceremony into her hot wetness, he instead slid himself between her thighs, gliding his length against her folds and the bottom of her clit, pushing himself forward until he felt the curve of her ass grazing the curls of his pubes.

The sawing motion had her moaning anew. Holding onto her hips, he teased her by pushing the head of his cock at her vagina, but instead of entering her, he slid along her folds. He knew his way around her pussy well, having spent a good amount of time admiring it, licking it, sucking it, fucking it. All the reasons for their break-up had dissolved. He only knew that he wanted her. Wanted her bad. Just the prospect of being inside her had him near coming.

"You gonna fuck me or what?" she demanded between heavy breaths.

He speared himself into her. *Incroyable.* She felt tighter than he remembered. But every bit as divine. He closed his eyes, lost in the most incredible place his body had ever known. When he was assured that he had control, he began thrusting. She writhed in delight. She liked being penetrated from behind, he knew. Her ass slapped against his pelvis as he drove himself deep within her. At times she was pushed onto her toes.

Reaching around her, he found her clitoris again with his hand. He trembled his fingers in short rapid motions against her. It sent her over the edge. She shook against him, her legs giving way beneath her. He wrapped his arm around her waist and held her up as he plunged his cock into her. His desire burst from him. Letting out a carnal roar, he bucked against her uncontrollably as his orgasm thundered through his body.

When his heart was no longer beating as if he had just sprinted the hundred meter dash, he pulled himself from her. A last shudder went through his body. He took in a big breath of the crisp winter air and planted a kiss on her shoulder. He wanted to wrap her in an embrace or carry her to the bed and lay with her as he caressed her nakedness. But such tenderness might jolt her.

Instead, he murmured, "That had better beat any fucking ice cream."

She mumbled something incoherent, so he took that as agreement. He noticed that the threesome, having finished what they were doing, stared up at them. Whipping off the condom, he tossed it in a wastebasket and zipped his pants before untying the ribbon from Audrey's wrists.

"Merry Christmas," he whispered with a parting kiss on her neck.

Leaving her to undo the blindfold herself, he slid from the room and made his way downstairs. The party was still in full swing, though fewer guests were dancing and more were copulating. He retrieved his jacket from the coat check and left the party before Blaine could corner him and ask questions.

3

Charlene finished off her rum and coke and put the glass back on the counter behind her. She looked around for Audrey, feeling a little guilty for not having stayed at her friend's side more. But Audrey was a grown woman. She didn't need a chaperone or an escort. And she understood Charlene Johnson was never a wallflower. There were too many hot men here at Trey's party. Speaking of hot men, where had Russell Wong gone off to?

"Need another drink? Carl here makes a tasty Long Island Iced Tea."

Charlene turned around and met the crystal blue eyes of Blaine Edwards, a player with beach boy good looks. There was a time when she would have done him, just for fun. She'd never slept with a blonde before. And he was about as good looking as they came. He dressed well, too, enough to suggest he might be a closet gay. Which would make him even more intriguing. But now that Audrey and Rance were broken up, Blaine was a no-no.

"Seriously?" Charlene replied with an arched brow. "That's a drink for hoes and men who need to get a girl drunk to get laid."

He winced. "Ouch."

But he wasn't fazed, and even in the dim lighting, she could see his eyes sparkle.

"Dragon fruit martini then?"

"Nah. I don't really do fancy drinks. I'm not a fancy girl. *And* I'm capable of getting my own drink."

His gaze swept over her briefly—it lasted barely a second—but Charlene caught the assessment. With a body like Beyonce's, she was used to men--and women--checking her out. She didn't even have her sexiest outfit on. Just a little red number with a sweetheart neckline and a hemline high enough to show off her shapely legs. Her *pièce de résistance* was a pair of shoes that laced all the way up her calves and over the knees.

"Those can't be comfortable," Audrey had said on first seeing the shoes. "And no wonder you're late. It probably took a half a day to get into those things."

Charlene had waved a dismissive hand. "Yeah, but they're worth it."

"Why do you even bother? You could probably score a dozen men just wearing sweats and flannels."

"Yeah, but it's more *fun* this way."

From the flicker of appreciation in Blaine's eyes, Charlene gathered he liked her shoes, too. She scanned the room behind him, looking for Audrey and Russell Wong.

"Boy, you don't make it easy for a guy to hit on you," Blaine said. He glanced at the empty glass behind her. "Rum and coke."

"If you want to get me a rum and coke, you're welcome to. But there's no guarantee I'll still be here when you get back," she said, flashing him a smile to soften the blow.

He whistled and shook his head. "A guy could interpret that as playing hard to get."

"Just trying to save you some time and trouble. I usually try to avoid getting drunk at these things. It's how stupid shit happens. Like finding naked photos of yourself on the internet. But if you need a bigger hint—"

He held up his hand. "I get the picture. But maybe I'm just dumb enough to keep trying."

She shrugged her shoulders and leaned against the counter. "You are a blonde."

He finished off the Maker's Mark in his hand and set it on the counter next to her glass. In doing so, he had taken a half step closer to her.

"If I were into BDSM and shit like that," he said, his voice a little huskier, "comments like that would get you a really nasty spanking."

She sucked in her breath.

He leaned in, his mouth beside her ear. "Something tells me you're a girl that likes a good spanking."

Her arm slipped off the counter. He caught her. Quickly, she removed her arm and straightened.

"Rance here?" she asked, pretending what he had said was as unprovocative as a comment about the weather.

"No. Tried to talk him into coming, especially when Trey told me you were bringing Audrey."

"Rance dating anyone?"

"A few dates with a woman named Stephanie. I don't think it's going anywhere, though. What about Audrey?"

Now that they were on a safer subject, Charlene relaxed. Blaine, too, had dropped his Casanova act.

"Not really," she answered. "I was kinda hopin' she'd hook up with someone here. Just for fun, you know. Make her forget about Rance. Especially since *he's* moved on."

"I thought they'd still be in touch, stay friends."

"Pain's still too raw, I guess."

"Yeah, but they're the mature ones, intellectual, compassionate, and all that good crap."

"Love screws everyone over."

"That's why I just like to screw."

Charlene couldn't help a chuckle. "They were good together, though. I thought they were going to make it."

"I did, too."

From the thoughtfulness in his voice, she could see that Blaine cared a lot about his friend.

"Well, tell Rance I said 'hi.'"

"Will do. Where's Audrey?"

"I have no idea. Probably hiding in the bathroom checking her email on her cell. I better go look for her."

"Merry Christmas."

He gave her a chaste peck on the cheek and let her go.

"Merry Christmas," she returned and headed for one of the bars set up in the living room. She was going to get herself another rum and Coke. Hopefully, it would dispel that spanking comment Blaine had made.

Blaine admired the view as Charlene walked away. Her hips didn't sway when she walked—some women did that hip sashay thing, thinking it made them look sexy, except it sometimes came off cartoonish, like Jessica Rabbit in that movie *Who Framed Roger Rabbit*—but something definitely happened when she walked, and it spoke directly to his groin. Maybe it was the way her butt cheeks, pushed up by her five-inch heels, moved in rhythm to her steps. And those shoes...*goddamn*. They were a bit over the top, downright slutty, really, but she pulled it off. Maybe because she openly admitted to being a sex fiend and didn't give a crap what people thought. That was the difference between Charlene and a slut: sluts had low self-esteem and though they thought sex would make them better or more likable, it usually had the opposite effect. But with Charlene, sex was empowering. And that made her hot as hell.

His comment about the whole BDSM thing was a gamble, but he saw—no, he had felt—her body tense. He figured someone like Charlene had tried just about everything under the sun. According to Trey, whose friend Damien had dated her for a while, Charlene hadn't ventured into BDSM, but Blaine hadn't detected anything in Charlene that would suggest she was repulsed by what he had said. He felt the blood churn around his cock thinking of her ass getting spanked. Holy shit. He'd pay money to see that. He'd pay double to be the one doing the spanking.

"Hey, I was going to hit on Charlene."

It was Trey, who had probably already fucked a girl before the party and another one—or two—during. In fact, he had his arm draped around a skinny young redhead. She either didn't hear what Trey had said or was too smashed to care. She giggled in between sips from a bottle of beer she held.

"What? You get dibs 'cause you're the host?" Blaine replied.

"It doesn't matter. I saw you strike out anyway."

"I don't know if she dates white guys."

"She's racist just cause she didn't dig your sorry ass?"

"Hiiiii," drawled the redhead to Blaine. "I'm Scarlet."

She held out her hand, but it was the one holding the bottle. Her other arm was wrapped around Trey's waist.

"Black people can't be racist," Blaine said.

"Why the hell not?"

"Would you want to date a race of people that enslaved yours for hundreds of years, beat you up, treated you like sub-par humans, and screwed with you every which whey they could—outside the law, inside the law, with the law?"

Trey jerked his head back. "When did you get to be so politically correct? Damn Stanford grad."

Blaine was mostly messing with Trey, who, not surprisingly, had gone to a party school.

"Tell you what," Trey said. "Being as I'm such a nice guy, if I get it on with Charlene, maybe I'll convince her to add you and a girl of your choosing for a foursome. You'd do the same, right?"

"You went to Stanford?" Scarlet asked. "You must be like, tooooootally smart."

Blaine looked from the young woman to Trey, then back to the young woman, whose chin suddenly jutted out as she hunched her shoulders.

"I think you better take her to the bathroom," he suggested. "Whatever she's been drinking is about to come up."

Trey's eyes widened, but he quickly ushered Scarlet away. Blaine leaned against the counter, trying to picture a foursome with Trey. Not that Trey wasn't good-looking. He resembled James Franco at the right angle. But Blaine wasn't all that into seeing another guy's goods. He wasn't against it, but why bother if you didn't have to? Now a foursome comprised of three women...that was another story. He had done a threesome before and it was every bit as awesome as he'd dreamed. But would three women be one too many? Unless two of them were going at it with each other, there was only so much of them that he could access. He supposed he could try to jack one off with his hand while one sat on his face and the other on his cock.

"Hey there, stranger."

A woman with black hair cut in a bob, wearing a black halter and black leather boots, sporting black nail polish and generally looking like she was at a Halloween party instead of a Christmas party, smiled at him. Beside her stood a platinum blonde wearing skin-tight pants and a white bandeau top. Both looked to be in their late-twenties. Both fairly hot babes. Blaine preferred the latter over the Goth-looking chic.

"My name's Montana," said the blonde.

"I'm Monica," said the other woman. "You like the party so far?"

"Yeah," Blaine replied. "Last year's was more naughty, though."

"Really? Maybe we can change your opinion on that."

Blaine remained nonchalant, though he was smiling inside. This was exactly why he came to the party. "Yeah?"

"We've been dating for a while," Montana said, looking at Monica. "Thought we'd spice up our love life with a little something, or someone, extra."

Bingo.

"You up for that, stranger?" Monica asked.

Blaine would have leaped over the barstools at the opportunity, but he played it cool and calm. "Happy to help you ladies out."

Straightening, he put an arm around each of their waists. A few minutes later, the three of them were ensconced in a room upstairs. Montana was beneath him on the bed as Blaine frenched her. He thought he smelled weed on her, but it didn't matter. People came to Trey's party for one primary reason: to fuck.

Monica worked herself out of her boots, then her dress. Blaine looked up without leaving Montana's mouth to admire Monica's slim body, now naked except for a lacey hip hugger and bra. He pulled the bandeau down to free Montana's pert little breasts. He grabbed a hold of one and licked the nipple. She moaned. He worked his mouth on the hardened bud, swirling his tongue around it, sucking it, licking it. She moaned again and arched her back. Monica positioned herself above Montana's head and pushed Blaine off of her.

"Let's get you undressed," she said.

Montana slid onto the floor and the two women worked simultaneously to divest him of his shirt and pants. His cock sprang to attention.

Monica eyed it with appreciation. "Commando?"

"It is a Naughty Noel," he answered.

Montana wrapped her mouth around him. She wasn't the best at giving head, but the warm moistness of her mouth felt good nonetheless. Monica flicked her tongue at his nipple. Despite the onslaught of sensations in all the right places, his thoughts wandered. Right to Charlene Johnson. He wondered if she was all show and no substance. Just because a woman was hot didn't make her good in bed. But Charlene was so hot, it really wouldn't matter. He wouldn't mind doing all the work.

Montana grabbed his balls and squeezed as she slurped him up. He was glad for the distraction. He didn't need to be thinking about Charlene too much.

4

I don't believe you."

"I don't believe *you,*" Audrey returned as she compared her salad of mixed greens to Charlene's cheeseburger and onion rings at a bistro near Charlene's apartment in the SoMa district. "You didn't make it with anyone at Trey's party?"

"I thought I'd turn gay before that happened," Charlene acknowledged as she dunked her onion ring into the ranch sauce and motioned for their server. "Maybe I didn't drink enough."

"I think I drank too much. No way I would've done what I did if I hadn't."

"Un-huh. I don't know. You got a kinky side, girl, admit it."

"Maybe you were so drunk you don't remember that you screwed someone."

"Yeah, I thought about that, too, but I'm pretty sure I was mostly sober." Charlene turned to the server. "Can I get more of the ranch dip? And I'll take another strawberry lemonade."

Audrey shook her head. "We just spent an hour working out. How can you eat that stuff?"

"I figure I just earned my calories at the gym."

"You may find a way to stay skinny—I think you got some defective genes or something because no one can be as skinny as your ass eatin' what you do—but you're gonna die early of heart disease or get type 2 diabetes. It's gonna catch up with you someday. Even the sex. Honestly, I think it's great you didn't make it anyone at Trey's party."

"Well, I tried. I had me a tasty kung-fu guy."

"What happened?"

"I think he got annoyed I kept calling him Russell when his name was Chen or Chang or something like that. Anyway, he ended up with some skanky blonde. And I end up with Trey trying to make the moves on me, thinking he can get some just 'cause he the host and shit."

Taking a bite of her unfulfilling salad, Audrey tried to pretend Charlene's cheeseburger with avocado and blue-cheese dressing didn't exist. "Why didn't you just bang Trey? He's good-looking."

"*Because*...that stereotype that our men are bigger and better in bed—you know what I mean—well, it's all true."

"You'd know, I suppose. You've slept with enough men to be able to conduct your own scientific study."

"Damn right. White men are kinda boring. But let's talk about you, you skanky hoe. So you have no idea who the guy was?"

"Probably better I didn't," Audrey replied as she watched the juices from the hamburger drip onto the plate as Charlene took another bite.

"You didn't get a look at him at all?"

"He was probably butt ugly. That's why he had to sneak up on me."

"I dunno. I think it's sexy. And he got you to come? Just how good was the orgasm?"

Audrey stopped chewing and looked up at the server who had just returned to the table with Charlene's extra ranch dip and lemonade.

"Can I get you ladies anything else?" he asked with a wry smile.

Audrey shook her head vehemently. Charlene looked him over. It was hard to tell, but he might have had some black in him.

"Maybe," Charlene said with her mouth half full of onion ring. "Why don't you check back in a couple of minutes?"

"Will do."

When he had left, Audrey glared at Charlene. "You could've said 'no.' Let's talk about something else."

"We're just talking normal adult stuff. It's not like we're gonna pull a Meg Ryan and fake an orgasm at our table. So, how was your orgasm?"

"Good, I guess. I was a little drunk."

"Did he leave a number?"

"Nope. Thank God."

"Why?"

"I don't want to see the guy again. What if he's somebody I know? What if he's somebody I don't like?"

"I don't think you and Trey have the same circle of friends."

"We know you. And what about acquaintances? What if he's someone I work with?"

"Like who?"

"I don't know. It could be anyone. You never know, right?" Audrey started feeling a little sick, thinking of all the people, many of them in public service, that she worked with. "What if he recognized me?"

"What did he sound like?"

"I'm guessing white, but I don't know for sure. He whispered most of the time. I was drunk, like I said. Shoot. That is the last time I let you drag me to one of your crazy parties. And I should stay away from alcohol unless it's a totally safe setting."

Feeling stressed, Audrey wondered if she ought to take a look at the dessert menu. She had ordered the light salad dressing, after all.

"I could ask Trey for his guest list."

"What about friends of guests?"

"Oh, right. I could ask him if he saw someone. Or I could ask Blaine. I saw him headed upstairs."

Audrey frowned. The same thought seemed to pass through Charlene's mind.

"He wouldn't," Charlene said seriously. "He respects Rance too much. Besides, he was with two other women. You know he tried to hit on me?"

"That's Blaine. What else is new?"

"Yeah." Charlene chewed her burger. "Only it was a little different this time."

"He said 'hello' first, before asking to fuck you."

"I don't think I even got a 'hello.' But that's okay. You know me. I like cutting to the chase. I don't know. It was just different."

"Good different?"

"Just different. He says 'hi,' by the way."

"Did he, uh, talk about Rance?"

"Not really. Just said he thought you and Rance were gonna go all the way. He even sounded kinda wistful about it."

Audrey took in a deep breath. Not that she wouldn't have been happy for Rance if Blaine had announced that Rance was engaged to the new love of his life, but she wasn't ready to hear it.

"Blaine's not a bad guy," she said. "Just abnormally oversexed. Kinda like someone else I know."

"Who? Me?"

The two women chuckled and finished their lunch.

"Dessert menu?" the server asked upon returning.

Audrey hesitated before replying, "I'll pass."

Charlene grabbed the last piece of onion ring before he cleared away the plates. "I never pass on looking at the dessert menu."

"You never pass on dessert, period."

"I hope they have one of those sample platters 'cause it's so hard to decide on dessert. Or I'll end up ordering two desserts, and I can't finish both. Most of the time."

Audrey shook her head. "No wonder I'm one of the few women friends you got. Other women gotta hate your ass."

The server returned with the dessert menu.

"I'll take a look, too," Audrey said.

After blowing her workout on a slice of chocolate torte with crème anglais, Audrey thought about going back to the gym. It was a Sunday and she didn't have much else going on. Sitting in her Russian Hill apartment, she reached for the remote control to the TV but paused when she heard people talking. A Spanish-speaking family had moved in next door, into the unit where Rance once lived. Sort of lived. Blaine would joke that Rance, who usually stayed in the penthouses of his hotels, had been "slumming it." The complex off Hyde Street was shaped like a duplex with two main entrances but with multiple units on each side. For a while, she had shared a wall with him without knowing. She smiled as she recalled how he had often cranked up his music, hoping to draw her out of her unit to talk to him in person. Instead, she had banged on the wall and shouted at him.

Thanks to the thin walls, he had overheard her calling an escort service, Pleasant Company, and took the place of her intended gigolo. What followed was the most magnificent sex and romance of her life. She was probably crazy to let him walk out of her life. He didn't have to, but he did. So maybe that meant he didn't love her as much as she had thought, or wanted, or needed. And as perfect as he might be in other areas, if he couldn't make room for her ambitions then he wasn't the right man for her.

Feeling hungry, she tried to avoid her refrigerator and went to retrieve some gum from her handbag. A copy of the *Nob Hill Gazette* fell out. It was the one with the photo of Rance and Stephanie at some fundraiser that cost a thousand dollars per head. Why had she put the darn thing in her purse? Unable to avoid the temptation, she opened the paper to the photo. They both had picture-perfect smiles. Rance was always the photogenic one between the two of them, but maybe he had found a better photo partner. They made a damn cute couple.

Audrey crumpled up the gazette and threw it into the wastebasket. It was definitely time to move on. She had allowed herself a grieving period. And though she may not be up for dating, maybe she could take a page out of Charlene's playbook and have a little fun.

"Does Trey throw other parties? Ones like the Naughty Noel?"

The cashew Blaine had tossed into the air bounced off his eye and hit Alan Chen, their friend and former roommate from college days.

"Say what?" Blaine asked Rance.

"Your friend Trey. Does he have another party planned? For New Year's Eve perhaps?" Rance said as he stuffed his hands into his coat pockets. The three of them were sitting at a 49ers game. He was mildly interested in the game of American football. What he wasn't interested in was sitting in the winter cold to watch it, but Blaine and Alan were both diehard fans and preferred to sit closer to the action rather than a luxury box.

"Trey still does his Naughty Noel?" Alan asked. "How come I didn't get invited?"

Blaine cocked a brow. "Because you're *married.*"

"So?"

"You don't do crazy shit when you're married."

"Says who?"

"First of all, even if you didn't have a ball and chain—don't get me wrong, if you had to have a ball and chain, Janine's an awesome choice and I'd do her in a heartbeat if you weren't in the picture—"

Alan shifted in his seat to face Blaine more fully. "Is that supposed to make me feel better?"

"I'm just sayin' Janine's cool—and hot."

"Just so you know, Janine wouldn't do it with you even if she wasn't married to me."

Rance shook his head. Poor Alan. Blaine always knew how to yank his chain.

"Fact is you wouldn't be going to Trey's party even if you were single. You're a US Attorney. You'd probably have to arrest half the guests. Not sure you'd want it on your resume that you were at the party anyway."

"Janine might have gone for it. Just because you're married doesn't mean you can't do kinky things."

Blaine leaned back and tossed up another cashew, catching it in his mouth. "Sure it does. Sex after marriage isn't the same."

"It gets better."

"Yeah? When was the last time you and Janine did the nasty?"

Alan shifted uncomfortably. "She's in her first trimester with a bad case of morning sickness."

"Un-hunh. You realize there's even less sex after baby comes?"

Rance stared at Blaine. "You speak from experience?"

"No. But I know a lot of MILFs. There's a reason housewives get desperate. Why do you want to know about Trey anyway?"

Rance looked out onto the football field, trying to remember if the 49ers were the ones wearing white or gold jerseys. "Maybe I'll go to the next one."

Blaine sat up. "Yeah?"

"Do you think...Audrey will be there?"

"You want to get back with Audrey?" Alan asked.

"I just want to see her."

"You can try something called email or the phone..."

Rance cleared his throat. "I had something else in mind."

"What about Stephanie?"

"We're not exclusive."

"Men and women see exclusivity differently."

"If you wanted to see Audrey, why didn't you go to the Naughty Noel?" Blaine asked.

"What just happened?" Rance evaded, eyeing the scoreboard. "How did they get two points?"

"A safety."

"You want to see Audrey, but you're not interested in getting back together?" Alan asked.

"Just because we're not together doesn't mean we're enemies," Rance said.

"And you *don't* want to get together again? You just want to be, what, friends? I don't quite follow."

"Are you always in lawyer mode?"

"Nah, I just like to be annoying."

"I'm not saying I don't want to be back with Audrey, but she made it pretty clear where she stands."

"Why don't you just let her have her career? I supported Janine when she made partner at her law firm."

"Maybe I'd feel differently if I was married to Audrey."

"Women gotta get that career stuff out of their system," Blaine seconded. "They gotta feel like they fulfilled the spirits of Alice Paul and Shirley Chisholm. Then, when their biological clocks get louder, they'll think to themselves, 'Shit, I gotta get married and make a baby.'"

"Let's just watch the game." Rance looked at the play clock. He couldn't remember if football had quarters or halves. Given there was nine minutes and counting, he hoped the latter.

"Hey, if you want to go to Trey's party, I support you, buddy. Trey and Chris do a New Year's Eve of Erotica. That would be in three and a half weeks. Chris hosts it on Treasure Island."

"I'd only go if I knew Audrey was going. Except she may not go if she knows I'm going, so she can't know."

"How are you going to know if Audrey goes to the party or not?" Alan asked as he stuffed more garlic fries into his mouth and washed it down with his beer.

Blaine perked up. "I can ask Charlene."

Rance figured that would be just about the only way to find out. The conversation was going better now. The truth was he would probably get back together with Audrey in a heartbeat. Stephanie was sweet and pretty, but she wasn't Audrey. And Audrey felt right to him. If only he could get her to see that he was right for her.

But he obviously wasn't, in her opinion. He was sure, however, that no one could pleasure her like he could. And while he would like to see her and talk with her, he also wanted to feel her. Be deep inside of her. Where only his cock had penetrated. He had another crazy idea, just like the time he had impersonated a gigolo. He'd probably have to admit his plan to Blaine or his friend might blow it, just like Blaine nearly blew his cover the first time he encountered Audrey, who had tried passing herself off as a woman named "Brittany." He smiled, recalling how tentative and awkward she had been that first day, probably regretting that she had called Pleasant Company to begin with. He had changed her mind soon enough. What he wouldn't give to do it all over again...

And it would seem an opportunity presented itself once more.

5

Charlene looked up from behind the receptionist counter at Stevenson & Young and narrowed her eyes at the blonde Ken doll leaning against the counter. "Just happened to be in the building?" she repeated in disbelief.

"Yep," Blaine replied. "I've got a friend who works for Rochester Banking downstairs. He wants me to invest in this new startup."

Charlene looked to see if Audrey was around, then remembered she was in a meeting with one of the new hires. "Then shouldn't you be on the fourteenth floor?"

He flashed a smile of perfectly white teeth. "The view's better up here."

Charlene rolled her eyes. "Is there anything with a pussy that you don't hit on or do you do them all: two-legged, four-legged..."

"As long as they're hot—and sassy—I don't care how many legs they have."

She tried unsuccessfully to suppress her smile. Blaine leaned in further.

"You able to get a coffee break?"

"Yeah, but I don't need or want any coffee right now."

"I've got a legitimate question, but it's private."

She gave him her sweetest smile. "I'm sorry, but the answer is no. I won't sleep with you, honey."

He straightened. "Given the number of guys you've slept with, I must be pretty offensive for you not to give me one shot."

She frowned. "You callin' me a slut?"

"No! I mean, if I was saying that, I'd be one, too. Hell, I am one. Why not own it? But what is it about me? You don't like my aftershave? You don't think white guys can rock it, too?"

"It's the hair. I like my men tall, *dark*, and handsome."

"I can dye it. Whaddya like? Purple? Orange?"

She couldn't help it. She laughed at the thought of Blaine with bright purple hair. "I'll think about it."

His smile broadened. "All right. Well, now that we're making some headway, how about that coffee break?"

"No, no. If I was gonna to sleep with you, I don't need a date."

"It's not a date. Like I said, it's a legitimate question and I'm just the messenger. The question's from Rance."

She sat up in her chair and looked around again for signs of Audrey. "Seriously?"

He held up his hand. "Scout's honor."

She grabbed her purse and placed a sign reading "Back in 15 minutes" on the counter.

"Okay, blondie, let's go."

They walked out of the office and headed to the elevators. She stole a glance at Blaine, wondering what he looked like naked. He had a good physique, and he looked pretty hot, for a white guy, in his button down shirt and khakis. Rich guys could get away with dressing casual. Poor Audrey had to don a suit every day.

"You work here long?" Blaine asked as they waited for the elevators.

"Five years."

"Like your job?"

"Why? You got an opening with your company?"

He watched the numbers light up as the elevator approached their floor. "No way in hell I'd hire you."

"Why the hell not? 'Cause I don't got no fancy degree like you or Audrey?"

"Because I'd want to fuck you every day," he said casually as the elevator doors opened. "Can't do business with that kind of distraction."

He swept his arm inward for her to go first. She didn't budge at first, but seeing that there were people waiting in the elevator, she quickly entered. The other two people in the elevator stood aside, then resumed their positions in front.

"Damn, boy, you just lay it out there, don't you?" she said beneath her breath.

He looked at her, his gaze smoldering. Small shivers went up her back.

"Maybe if you didn't look so damn hot all the time…"

The other two people turned their heads slightly. Blaine had not bothered lowering his voice. His gaze raked over her. As the receptionist for Stevenson & Young, a public finance firm, Charlene had more leeway to dress the way she wanted to. She liked high heels and tight skirts. At the moment she was sporting a dark purple sweater with a scoop neckline that showed just a hint of cleavage, a knit skirt, and black leather boots with silver buckles.

"…I wouldn't be thinking of all the different positions I could try with you," he finished.

One of the elevator occupants, a short man with a receding hairline, huffed in disgust. "Can you keep that to yourself?"

The elevator doors opened and the other two quickly exited.

Charlene shook her head at Blaine. "You're worse than me."

"Don't let it bother you. I know that guy. He's an attorney with Mason and McAllister. Total dick."

They walked over to the coffee shop on the ground floor of the office building.

"I'll take the mocha-caramel-choco-chip freeze with extra whipped cream," Charlene ordered. She looked over the display case of baked goods. "Ooooh. That Oreo brownie cake stack looks good. I'll try one of those."

Beside her, Blaine's eyes widened. "You order like that all the time?"

"Yeah, why?"

"That's enough calories for an NFL lineman. And that stuff'll clog your arteries."

"What are you? Some kind of health freak? You one of those vegetarians?"

"Coffee. Black," Blaine told the clerk before turning his attention back to her. "I like my burgers and steak as much as the next man. But all good things in moderation."

She allowed him to pay for her order. "Except sex, right?"

"Do you know of any side effects from too much sex?"

"Audrey thinks there's gotta be something. Maybe bad knees. You can't get arthritis in your penis, can you?"

He laughed. "There are no joints in a penis."

She shrugged as they sat down at a small table. "Then I don't think there is anything. I got a cramp in my leg once trying to ride a guy who couldn't come."

"Couldn't come?"

"Yeah, he put some crazy shit on his dick, something to make him last longer. Except it musta dulled the sensations in his penis."

"I almost got a concussion having sex."

"Yeah?"

"It was at this woman's place, in her bedroom. The bed kept hitting the wall. Finally the shelf above the bed gave way. She had this marble Buddha on it. The damn thing fell right on my head."

She stifled a laugh. "Sorry."

"Guess sex can be an extreme sport."

A server set her drink and dessert in front of her. She wrapped her mouth on the straw and took a long draw of the mocha-caramel-choco-chip freeze. It was like a party in her mouth.

Across from her, Blaine shook his head. He leaned back in his chair. "I'd like to be the guy you fuck after having one of those."

"You wouldn't be able to handle it. Trust me."

With her finger, she scooped a dollop of the whipped cream, drizzled with chocolate and caramel sauce and topped with chocolate flakes, into her mouth. She closed her eyes, savoring the taste. When she opened her eyes, he was staring at her, and the irises of his eyes seemed to have melted.

"Now you're just teasing me," he said and deliberately shuddered. "Look, I wanted to talk to you about the New Year's Eve of Erotica. Are you going?"

"Haven't decided. I might have other plans."

Truth was she didn't want to end up with another dud like she had at the Naughty Noel.

"Rance might go."

"Really?"

"If Audrey goes."

"Not likely. She's all wierded out by what happened at the Naughty Noel."

"What happened?"

"None of your business."

"I'm surprised she went in the first place."

"Me, too. I'm glad she did, though."

"You think you can convince her to go to the Eve of Erotica?"

"You hearing me, blondie? Besides, if Rance wants to see her, why doesn't he just call her or stop by?"

He stared into his coffee. "I'm not sure. Maybe, given how they started out, he's looking to reconnect in a...unique way."

She perked up, and not just because she now had a sugar high. "So he's still interested in Audrey?"

"Yeah. Just because the relationship is over doesn't mean he's fallen out of love with her. After all, she was the one who dumped him."

"It wasn't like that. He walked out on her."

"Guess it was a mutual disengagement. But I can tell he misses her."

"What about that European model he's dating? I saw her picture in the paper."

"Stephanie? Don't think there's enough chemistry there." He leaned across the table. "Rance and Audrey were good together. I figure if there's an opportunity, a second chance for them, and we can help facilitate it, why not?"

Food made Charlene think better, so she forked the layered cake and broke off a large bite. She liked Rance. She liked him for Audrey. How happy he made her. How well he cared for her. Sometimes she wondered if Audrey thought he was too good to be true, and maybe Audrey pushed him away because she didn't believe in the dream.

"Okay, but I don't think I can get Audrey to go to another party. She wasn't sure about the Naughty Noel."

Blaine smiled. "I have a feeling what Charlene Johnson wants, Charlene Johnson gets."

"Audrey's a little more resistant to my charms than people who have a penis."

He glanced at his cell phone. "Look, I gotta run to my next meeting. But you get Audrey to the Eve of Erotica, I promise I won't try to score with you anymore. That's how far I'm willing to go for Rance. Audrey, too, if she knows what's best for her. Just don't tell her that Rance is going."

"And if I don't get her to go? I mean, you know Audrey. Shit, I still can't believe she took me up on that Pleasant Company gift card I gave her."

He stood up and said, almost business-like, "Then you owe me a date. I'll take you to Ballander's."

Her eyes widened. Ballander's was a fairly new restaurant and one of the few in the Bay Area to receive three Michelin stars. "The one in Healdsburg?"

"Is there another?"

"You can't get a reservation there for months."

"They book four months out," he conceded. "But I'll get us in."

She looked at him as if he had just promised her the moon. "Because you're so damn charming?"

"Because I'm one of the original investors with partial ownership. Text me when you hear from Audrey."

With a final smile, he left. Charlene stared at her mocha-caramel-choco-chip freeze. What the hell just happened? How did she end up in an either-or situation with Blaine? And a possible date with him for that matter? Though, for the chance to dine at Ballander's... And it wasn't like Blaine was this ugly, disgusting guy. He was hunky, a little funny, and about as easy going with sex as she was. Maybe this wasn't a bad deal. Get Audrey to the Eve of Erotica and she wouldn't have to deal with Blaine hitting on her anymore—though she wasn't a hundred percent sure she could trust him to stop, but it couldn't hurt to try. Don't get Audrey to the Eve of Erotica and she'd get to eat for free at one of Northern California's most exclusive restaurants. It was a win-win.

Satisfied, she dug her fork into the Oreo brownie cake stack for another large bite.

"So what is it you're hoping will happen at the Eve of Erotica?" Blaine asked as he looked over the renderings for the remodel of the restaurant in *Hotel Sur Mer*, one of the boutique hotels owned by the Durand family.

Sitting opposite him in the lounge area of the restaurant, Rance put another portfolio of sketches before Blaine. "Maybe nothing."

"I got a right to know. I just promised Charlene that if she got Audrey there, I'd stop trying to hook up with her. That's a pretty big sacrifice."

"You weren't going to get anywhere with Charlene anyway."

"Thanks for the vote of confidence, bro."

Rance reached for his glass of water and sat back in the leather seat. "It may seem like Charlene sleeps with everyone, but Audrey told me she has standards."

Blaine stared. "Are you my fucking friend or what?"

"Sorry. You know I didn't mean it like that."

Blaine waved a hand. "Just joshin' you. I know you'd sleep with me in a heartbeat if you could. But I gotta wonder, 'cause Charlene does get around, why won't she do it with me? Just for kicks."

"Maybe you get around too much. Maybe she's looking for a relationship. She's had steady boyfriends before."

"She's had sex-mates before. I'm not sure they're boyfriends in the classical sense."

"I think you're wrong. I think women prefer to have relationships over meaningless sex."

"Yeah, but Charlene's a different animal. There's got to be a way. You think she likes diamonds?"

"That's offensive."

"You sound like Alan."

"You want her to prostitute herself."

"She wouldn't see it like that. She'd see it as a...sensible exchange. Something she wants for something I want."

Rance blinked several times. "How are we friends?"

Blaine didn't hear the question. He was too busy thinking about the potential date to Ballander's and how he could work that angle. He hadn't planned on making a bet, of sorts, with Charlene. It had happened before he knew it. She could have just declined. But she hadn't. Truth was, he didn't think he stood much of a chance getting in her pants so the promise of not hitting on her wasn't a stretch. But if she didn't come through with Audrey, maybe his chances weren't so bleak.

"Are you going to put in the two million for the kitchen or not?" Rance asked.

"Sure, but you got to tell me what you're up to with Audrey first."

Rance took a deep breath. "I bumped into her at the Naughty Noël."

"You were there?"

"Except she didn't know it was me."

"Go on."

"I saw she was a little drunk, a little…aroused at what she was seeing. So I snuck up behind her, wrapped a blindfold over her eyes, and…pleasured her."

Blaine stared at his friend wordlessly for a minute before saying, "You are a sick fuck."

"I guess I shouldn't have—"

"Dude, I'm kidding. That's awesome! You are the man! Now don't go guilt-trippin' yourself because that's what Trey's Naughty Noel is all about. You naughty, kinky bastard. I knew there was a reason I loved you."

Rance let out a breath. "You're ecstatic approval makes me wonder if I did the right thing."

"Did she come?"

"What does it matter?"

"If she did, then she liked it. She *enjoyed* it."

"Doesn't mean she didn't wake up with regrets."

"Well, you'll know if she shows up at the Eve of Erotica."

"That's what I'm thinking. Otherwise, I owe her an apology for taking advantage of her drunken state."

"So, were you thinking of doing the same thing at the Eve of Erotica?"

"No, not exactly. I don't want her drunk. I want her to be lucid, fully aware of what she's doing."

"But you're still gonna be the shadow lover?"

Rance had a half-smile. "I think the anonymity excites her. Like it did before. Besides, she wouldn't do anything if she knew it was me."

"You sure about that?"

"Too much emotionally at stake if it was us. But if it's all anonymous—or at least it is on her side—it's just sex. Naughty, kinky sex."

Blaine nodded. "That's what I'm talkin' 'bout!"

He flipped through the renderings once more, then wondered if he could pull a similar stunt with Charlene.

6

Dressed in her bathrobe, Charlene looked at her drawer full of vibrators and dildos, but today the sheer volume of choices overwhelmed her. She liked all her toys, liked the way they made her feel. She used them often. They were better and more effective than men in many, many instances. But she wanted to feel hot and horny. She didn't get *wet* for a toy. Blowing out her breath, she picked up a basic clit massager. It was a simple handheld vibrator, like the very first sex toy she had ever owned. It worked off a single double-A battery.

Taking it into bed with her, she turned it on and applied it to her clit. She thought about the Eve of Erotica. Damn it, if she was going to go, she was going to get some action at that thing. Normally, she would attend these types of events with someone she was dating or interested in. She wasn't afraid to go stag, or with Audrey, but the fact that she had come away from the Naughty Noel with nothing to show concerned her. She had no target, no beefcake she had set her sights on. What if she didn't come across anyone she liked?

She turned the vibrator onto a faster setting. The image of Blaine Edwards flitted through her mind. He'd be at the Eve of Erotica. He didn't seem to be seeing anyone. He liked her. She shook her head and dismissed the idea as quickly as it came. Although she didn't mind a fling, deep down she wanted a boyfriend. Not to settle down with and make a family, but a man to have crazy, wild sex with. To have fun together and enjoy all the benefits of being in a relationship: camaraderie, security, and even love. Finding someone new to fuck all the time was tiring. Edwards was not relationship material. He might be good for one or two nights, but that was about it. And she did not want to be a notch on his bedpost.

She thought about Damien, her last boyfriend. God, could he get it on in bed. His cock was big and it lasted a loooong time. But he wasn't as adventurous as she had hoped. In fact, he even seemed a little frightened by her. He hadn't even wanted to go to a titty-bar with her. He used to go to them with his buddies. She would have thought most guys would've died and gone to heaven at the suggestion. How many girlfriends would go there with their man, right? He should've got down on his knees and thanked the Lord for sending him such a magnificent girlfriend. Frustrated, she ground the vibrator into her clit. It got her to come, but the orgasm felt small. Damn.

Reaching for her cell on the bedside table, she called up Audrey.

"Hey, girl, watcha doin' New Year's Eve?" she asked.

Charlene would've bet money the answer would fall into one of the following categories: Nothing, Working, Hanging at my folks' place, Watching TV, or Sleeping.

"Nothing," Audrey replied.

"Great. 'Cause I got something even more fun than the Naughty Noel."

Silence on the other end.

"This really cool chick, Chris, hosts this party called the New Year's Eve of Erotica. She does it with Trey. It's on Treasure Island, and I actually missed out on it last year because of Damien, so I'm going this year."

"Don't tell me you need a date?"

"I *want* to go with you."

"Un-huh. You want a designated driver."

"You know I don't drink at these things. Much. And I could get a cab if I needed. Chris's father runs a cab company, so there's plenty there."

"I don't know. There's an opening in the Fort Lauderdale office for a managing partner. If I can get one more new account, I think I have real good shot at it."

"Florida? You seriously would consider going to Florida? Honey, that's not a good state for black folk."

"What are you talking about? There's a sizable population of African Americans in Florida."

"You heard how they're treated? Black people are only good for the Orange Bowl there. Hell, even their pro athletes gotta deal with racist shit."

"That happens everywhere."

"More in Florida."

"It's ten o'clock at night, and I got a client meeting at eight in the morning. What are you really calling about?"

"The Eve of Erotica. You should go."

"I don't know anyone at these things, except you, and you were gyrating with Russell Wong most of the time."

"Okay, I promise I won't leave you unless you want me to. And I think you will. 'Cause I think your mystery man will be at the Eve of Erotica."

There was a pause, then Audrey said, "You can't know for sure."

"I could maybe find out. Would you go if he was?"

Another pause.

"What if Rance comes to this one?" Charlene tried. "Blaine's going."

"No. I do *not* want to go if Rance is going."

"Why not?"

"I have to explain that one to you? Would you go if Damien were going?"

"It wouldn't stop me."

Audrey sighed. "I just...we haven't seen each other in a while. I don't want our first encounter post break-up to be at some kind of sex-fest."

"Fine. But if you're seriously considering Florida, you should go to the Eve of Erotica because you won't have the chance to do so in Florida. The KKK there will burn it down."

Charlene could hear Audrey's exasperation.

"So you comin' with me or not?" she pressed. "Because I know you're just gonna be watching the countdown on TV if you don't."

"All right. I'll go. I mean, I'll think about it."

"Great. We can talk costumes tomorrow."

"Costumes?!"

"See you after the meeting."

With a smile, Charlene hung up. She thought about what Blaine had promised if she got Audrey to attend. But then she'd miss out on Ballander's. Hmmmm. How badly did she want to go to Ballander's?

Audrey stared at her cell phone. *That crazy Charlene.* She put the phone down and climbed into bed. It was still kind of early and she thought about turning on the television. Rance didn't like having a television set in the bedroom—granted, there wasn't much of a need for one with him—but it was the first change she made after he had moved out. Usually at this time of night she'd tune into Comedy Central, but she didn't feel like TV tonight. She felt...horny. She was in about two weeks from her period, i.e. her peak fertility, so that's probably why she was feeling more agitated than usual. She thought about the vibrator she kept in the drawer of her bedside table beneath books and magazines. It was silly. No one lived with her so she wasn't sure why she felt the need to hide it. When she was with Rance, he would sometimes use it on her. It wasn't even really a vibrator. It was a massager originally intended for use on sore muscles.

What the hell. She pulled it out, turned it on, and slipped it into her pajama pants. It hummed pleasantly between her legs. Of course it was a lot sexier when Rance held it. She wondered how long she would have to rely on the massager, and if she would need to venture into other sex toys just to keep things interesting. Though she was still nervous about what had happened at the Naughty Noel, she was intrigued by the thought of bumping into that guy again, maybe at that Eve of Erotica. Would he want to do something again with her? What would he do? She replayed the scene of the Naughty Noel over and over in her head. Soon, she was gasping and jerking against the massager. She let out a contented sigh. She needed that.

But she also wanted more.

She was half serious about going to the Eve of Erotica, but what was up with the costumes? Although, on second thought, maybe costumes weren't such a bad idea. She would be less recognizable. If she was so worried about being identified, she shouldn't have gone to the Naughty Noel. She was banking on not knowing anyone there except Charlene and Blaine. And she actually trusted Blaine. Rance wouldn't have him for a friend if he were a total jerk. But could she take that same chance at another crazy sex party?

Putting away the massager, she reached for her portfolio containing her notes for tomorrow's meeting. She had already reviewed the materials and gone over the main discussion points, but it didn't hurt to look it over one last time.

She reviewed it a third time the following morning on the train ride to the client's office out in the East Bay. The City of Pleasant Creek wanted to do a forward refi, and it wasn't something that she had a lot of experience in. She arrived at the city hall early and was waiting in the lobby for the city's finance director when a middle-aged, good-looking black man dressed in a nicely tailored suit walked up to her.

"Audrey Jones?" he asked.

She wondered if she should know the guy. He looked vaguely familiar.

"Yes."

He held out his hand. "Roy Miller, from the DC office."

They shook hands. "DC office?"

"I missed the annual company retreat—was in the middle of a divorce—but I heard good things about you, Ms. Jones."

"What are you doing out here?" she asked.

"I've done a lot of forward bonds, so Ainsley thought I could help out. You're still the lead, obviously, but I am at your disposal."

"Oh. Great."

He had such a deep, suave voice. A little like Morgan Freeman. But with a faint Southern drawl. It was sexy.

"I've only done one of these, so it's good to have you aboard," she said, wishing she didn't sound so formal and white.

But he gave her an easy-going smile. In her mind, she began calculating how long he might have been divorced. The company hosted a retreat once a year for senior-level personnel. It took place in February. He could be divorced a good half a year then.

"You didn't miss much at the retreat," she said. Divorce was such a tricky topic, she didn't want to touch it, but since he had put it out there, it was kind of like the elephant in the room.

"How long you been with Stevenson & Young?" she asked instead.

"Twelve years." He handed her his card.

The receptionist told them the finance director was ready to meet with them, and Audrey had to focus on the task at hand. But she hoped that Roy would be headed back to the Stevenson & Young office afterwards. Lucky for her, he had a rental and offered to drive her back to the office after the meeting.

"I'm glad you were in that meeting," Audrey said as Roy drove down Highway 24 back toward the city. "I didn't think to question their choice of Reyes and Reyes because they do all their bonds with them."

"I get the appeal of working with a boutique investment firm, but their experience with forward bonds is extremely limited. It shows in the pricing," Roy said.

"How long you staying out here?"

"Just two days, but conference me in on all the meetings you have. I'll probably be out here again in a month."

Audrey rejoiced a little. She liked his demeanor, and he was a handsome man. She always liked the look of a man in a good suit. Rance was always more casual and rarely donned a suit unless he was meeting with one of his Asian investors.

She and Roy talked about the usual first conversation topics: where he lived, what he did before working for Stevenson & Young, where he'd gone to college. She found out he had graduated from Georgetown with a degree in political science, worked as a Congressional Aide then at the Congressional Budget Office before being recruited to join Stevenson & Young.

"It's a diverse firm," Audrey noted of their company.

"'Course Ainsley is white, but a lot of the managing partners are people of color. I wonder what it's like to live in a city with more black folk."

Roy chuckled. "It's good and bad."

He then asked her the same questions. She told him she grew up in Richmond, a city with a sizable black population, then went to UC Berkeley. Her father was a custodian and her mother a social worker. She worked at an accounting firm for a year after college and was bored to tears. Then she tried a couple different things, including clerical positions, before a former classmate told her about a job opening at Stevenson & Young.

"They make you go through the summer training program?" Roy asked.

"Yeah, I was the oldest person in a room full of fresh college graduates. Thought the company was crazy when they told me they didn't have mouses for their computers."

"Slows you down."

"Yeah, who knew typing was so much faster than using a mouse? But it took me a month to believe it."

It was easy talking to Roy, and they reached the Financial District all too soon for Audrey. He balked at the price of parking in the nearest parking garage.

"Jesus, you could feed a family for weeks at that price," he muttered as he took the ticket from the machine. "Good thing I get to expense this."

"You want to expense a cup of coffee before we head up?" she asked.

"I'd like to, but I got another meeting in San Jose to attend."

Audrey wondered what time his meeting in the

South Bay was. Maybe he'd come back to the office and would be up for drinks afterwards.

When they entered the office, Charlene perked up in appreciation at seeing Roy. He introduced himself to her with that affable smile then went in to talk to Roger, one of the managing partners.

"He a regular prince charming," Charlene said to Audrey. "I got goose bumps just listening to him say 'Morning.'"

"Yeah," Audrey agreed. "He's got a sexy voice. He sat in on my meeting this morning."

"Oooh. How distracting."

"He could probably recite the multiplication table and I'd melt in my shoes."

Charlene eyed her friend. "You interested, Ms. Jones?"

"Nah. He lives in DC. Recently divorced, too."

"So?"

"I don't know that I'm ready for anything. At least not a commitment."

"Who says Roy isn't thinking the same thing? Especially after a divorce."

"Maybe I'll see if he wants to do something after work. Maybe get dinner at someplace more interesting than his hotel."

"Do it. 'Cause if you don't, I will. I could just sit and listen to him read the menu all night. Oh! But if he's not up for anything, we could go shopping for your costume instead."

"My what?"

"For the Eve of Erotica. It's kind of like the Exotic Erotic. People dress up."

"Nothing fancy, I hope?"

"It varies. But it's part of the fun."

"I didn't say I was going."

"Yes, you did."

Audrey gave Charlene a look that her grandmother used to give her as a child when she protested she hadn't taken a lick of frosting off the cake when in truth she had.

"You did!" Charlene insisted.

Shaking her head, Audrey went into her office, feeling a little more invigorated than usual.

7

Sitting in the hotel room that he used for his temporary residence, Rance stared at Audrey's name on his cell phone. He should call her, just to see how she was doing. Maybe she would be up for getting coffee. It was the holidays. People tended to get more sentimental this time of year. He knew he was. Staying at his hotel didn't help because this was where they had made love for the first time. Upstairs in the penthouse. Fuck. It had been the most exciting sex he had ever had since losing his virginity. And much more fulfilling. Closing his eyes, he remembered everywhere they had fucked, from the showers where he had buried his cock in her ass, to the room on the fourth floor where he had bent her over an open window.

He hated staying at his hotel, located on a cliff overlooking the Pacific, but he hadn't put much effort into finding a place. He had hoped that maybe the break-up with Audrey wasn't going to last, but when it became apparent that it was, he found himself in the middle of renovating the restaurant and having to find a new head chef since the old one had been lured away to be the head chef at Ballander's. He could have his personal assistant look for a place, but he was too particular about where he lived to trust someone else to find him a new home.

He had a flight back to France in a couple of days to spend two weeks with his family for Christmas. He was looking forward to seeing his parents, his sister, and especially his nieces. They were growing up so fast, morphing from girls to little ladies far too quickly. But he would have preferred to have Audrey with him. His family had only met her once before. They were eager for him to marry and start a family of his own, so they were happy to meet her. Now they had their hopes pinned on Stephanie.

He would miss Christmas with Audrey. He'd miss making the rounds donating food to the churches and soup kitchens and the toys to the nonprofits. He'd even miss sitting through the long sermons at Audrey's old Baptist Church in Richmond. He had bought her Christmas gift already, a pair of Tahitian black pearl earrings surrounded by small diamonds. He had seen her eying them on the only vacation they had taken together, in Kauai. Audrey wasn't an extravagant woman, so she didn't buy them and she wouldn't let him buy them for her. Though he wasn't an extravagant person either, he had the feeling his wealth made her uncomfortable.

The earrings were in the safety deposit box in the office. He should give them to Audrey. The earrings didn't do him any good, and he didn't feel right gifting them to anyone else. Therefore, he should call her up, see how she was doing, and give her her Christmas gift. It was just after five o'clock. She'd probably still be at the office, so he selected her work number and watched as his cell dialed the number.

"Stevenson & Young."

"Hi, Charlene, it's Rance."

"Rance! Hi!"

"Merry Christ—I mean, Happy Holidays."

"You don't have to worry about that PC stuff with me. I celebrate Christmas. Not a nameless holiday. Not Kwanzaa. Christmas."

"Merry Christmas then."

"Merry Christmas! How you doing?"

"Good. Is, uh, Audrey there?"

"No, she just left."

That was early for Audrey.

"All right," he said. "I'll try her on her mobile."

"Oh, uh, well..."

"What's the matter?"

"She's in a, kind of, meeting."

There was a pregnant pause.

"Charlene, what are you covering up?"

"She went out for drinks with a colleague. From out of town. Company office in DC. It's just that, if they're at a bar, it'll be noisy, she won't hear your call. You're probably better off trying her later."

Audrey rarely went out for drinks. And the fact that Charlene was obviously nervous was a dead giveaway.

"Ok, I'll do that," he said.

"Hey, Blaine says you're going to the Eve of Erotica party."

"I might."

"Pff. You and Audrey are so alike…I mean…"

"Tell me more about this colleague from DC."

The words were out of his mouth before he could consider the wisdom of going down that route.

"It's nothing. He just flew in yesterday."

"Is he single?"

"I think. Maybe. Why? You jealous?"

He had to hand it to Charlene. She may not be good at lying, but she had some good retorts.

"I just wanted to wish Audrey a Merry Christmas," he said, hoping it wasn't obvious that he was jealous.

"I'll tell her you called."

"No. That's not necessary. I can try her mobile."

"Well, I'm going to the Eve of Erotica for sure. Maybe I'll see you there."

"Yes, well, Merry Christmas."

After he hung up, he racked his memory for any mention of a colleague in DC. He didn't remember any. Not that it mattered. The guy could have been from Saturn. It didn't lessen the jealousy. Of course he wanted Audrey to find happiness, even if it meant with someone else. Nonetheless, the idea of her with another guy wasn't an easy thing to swallow. It meant she was definitely moving on. And why not? He had. Audrey might even be aware of Stephanie. He had not proactively sought to enter the dating scene. Stephanie had been assisting with a charity event that was to take place at the *Hotel Sur Mer*. They ended up talking about a few things over drinks. That led to her asking him if he wanted to catch the opening of *La Boheme* at the SF Opera.

He had second thoughts about his ideas for the Eve of Erotica. But if Audrey showed up, he was now determined to go through with it.

Charlene let out a sigh as she put the phone down. Now *that* was an awkward call. Why did Rance have to call today? At this hour? If he had called just ten minutes earlier, she could have put him through to Audrey. Instead, she had to fumble through the call, unsure of where her allegiance was. She liked Blaine's idea of getting the two back together, but if it wasn't meant to be, then Audrey was better off moving on sooner rather than later. And Roy seemed like a darn good catch. Course it was too early to tell. She was dying to know how it was going between Audrey and Roy right now. Too bad he had to go back to DC so soon.

As she gathered her stuff to head back home, she wondered if she should call her ex to wish him a Merry Christmas. No. She wasn't interested in getting back together with Damian. But she didn't feel like going home yet. She had already done her Zumba class in the morning, though there was another class in half an hour. She could go shopping for her costume for the Eve of Erotica, but she had told Audrey they would do that together.

For some reason, the idea of calling Blaine popped into her head. She didn't know where that came from, except maybe because she had just gotten off the phone with Rance. She shook her head. She wasn't thinking right. Maybe she needed to finish her Snickerdoodle from the afternoon.

Feeling better after having the cookie, she headed for her apartment. She spent the evening browsing the Internet, looking for ideas for her costume. She had a pretty good idea of what she was going to go for. After dinner, she took a bubble bath and read a few pages of the latest erotica she had downloaded onto her reader. Still in her towel, she decided to have a fudge popsicle. Reading always made her hungry or horny.

Her cell phone buzzed. She had a mouthful of fudge but she picked up the call anyway.

"Ar-een," she answered.

"Who's this guy from DC?"

She swallowed, then shivered as the large cold lump slid down her throat. "Blaine?"

"Did Audrey ask him out?"

"How do you know? Did Rance go crying to you about it?"

"No. He beat the shit out of me in squash. I didn't win a single set. So what's the story?"

Charlene took another bite of her popsicle, partly to give herself time to think. "I 'old Ransh all I know."

"What are you eating?"

"'Ud 'osicle." She swallowed. "Fudge popsicle."

There was a pause. "What'd you have for dinner?"

"Pasta alfredo from Lean and Quick Meals."

"That frozen shit you throw in the microwave? It's loaded with sodium."

"So? Tastes good."

"'Cause it's loaded with sodium."

"It's nonfat."

"That's why they load it with sodium. There's no flavor otherwise."

"Look, Mr. Health Freak—"

"It's simple health. Don't you listen to Michelle Obama?"

"What? Just 'cause I'm black I gotta do everything she does?"

"A third grader knows to eat better than you."

She glared at her phone. "I'm about to hang up on you, boy."

"Someone's got to straighten out your eating habits."

"You take me to Ballander's every day, I promise I'll give up on the Lean and Quick Meals."

"Speaking of Ballander's, you get Audrey to commit to the Eve of Erotica?"

"Not yet, but she ain't say 'no' yet." She had a sudden inspiration. "How about you take me to Ballander's if she says 'yes.'?"

"Instead of promising I won't hit on you anymore?"

"On top of."

"Then what do I get if she doesn't go?"

"You get to take me to Ballander's, like you said."

"So either way you get to go Ballander's?"

"That's the idea. You a smart cookie, Blondie."

"I take you to Ballander's *and* you go on a diet for one week."

"You sayin' I'm fat?"

"No, not that kind of diet. It's *my* diet. A diet that won't lead you to having a stroke before you're thirty."

"I made it to thirty last year."

"Final offer, darling."

Charlene pouted. "So, I get to go to Ballander's either way, but if I can't get Audrey to go to the Eve of Erotica, I gotta do your diet thing."

"Yep."

She pouted again. She supposed she should eat better. Audrey had said the same. And it would only be for a week. She could go back to her food afterwards.

"Fine."

"So what's the deal with this guy from DC? I thought we agreed we were getting Rance and Audrey back together."

"Yeah, it's a nice idea, but—"

"But nothing. Long distance relationships don't work out."

A little irritated at his demeanor, she replied, "Well, if Audrey gets the promotion in the Fort Lauderdale office, she'll be a lot closer to DC."

"She's up for a promotion?"

"There's an opening. No way to say right now."

"All the more reason we got to make this thing with Rance happen."

"I just want Audrey to be happy."

"If she's with Rance, she'll be happy."

"You know what I mean. And I think you're getting worked up over nothing. It's just drinks. She barely knows the guy." She leaned against the counter.

"But she asked him out for drinks?"

"He's visiting. She's just being nice. He flies back in a few days anyway. And it's not like Rance is just sitting around. We saw his picture in the society pages with that skinny-ass white girl."

"Audrey knows about Stephanie?"

"Hell, yeah."

"Look," he said after a long pause, "I want to get them this chance. If it doesn't lead anywhere, it's on them. If you get Audrey to the Eve of Erotica, I'll take you to Ballander's every month for the next year."

"That's a sneaky way to get twelve dates."

"I'll get you a gift certificate. You can take whomever you want."

Charlene held her breath. "You serious?"

"Do you like your mocha-caramel-choco-chip freeze?"

"Shit. Ok. I'll do it. I'll get Audrey to the Eve of Erotica. Maybe I'll offer to take her to Ballander's with me."

"And it won't hurt if you can keep that DC guy outta the picture till then. Is he a good looking fucker?"

"Pretty darn sexy."

"So is the dessert menu at Ballander's."

"Ok. I got it. I got it."

After hanging up, Charlene took in a deep breath. A whole year's worth of dining at Ballander's! She wanted to squeal. She would definitely invite Audrey to go with her. But she couldn't bribe Audrey with a dinner at Ballander's. Audrey would want to know how she got a reservation in the first place and how she could afford to go there. Well, Audrey was already open to the idea of going to the Eve of Erotica. Maybe just a little nudge was required. Looking at the time, Charlene realized Audrey was probably back home from having drinks with Roy…unless things went really well. She dialed Audrey.

"What's up, Charlene?" Audrey asked.

Hmmm. She didn't sound post-coital.

"You at home?"

"Yeah."

"So how did it go with Roy?"

8

Audrey stared at her latte, too nervous to drink it. A chocolate chip wheat germ cookie, her new favorite cookie at Specialty Café, her favorite bakery, sat uneaten. Rance had called yesterday, asking to get-together for coffee. Surprised to hear from him, she had agreed without thinking. She wanted to see him, but it was so much easier *not* to see him. She missed him, but she had to *stop* missing him. So would this get-together over coffee help or hinder things? He had sounded casual enough, friendly enough, which was to be expected. They were mature adults, and it wasn't as if either one of them had committed a crime. Unless withdrawing from one's partner and hiding in a job was a crime.

She had to be at the office within the hour, so there was a ready-made excuse in case things got awkward. She had checked herself in the mirror half a dozen times to see that she looked good. Her outfit, a white pantsuit over a black lace camisole, was a relatively new one and sharp looking. The shimmery cherry lipstick was also a new color she was testing out. And she had just gone to the stylist, so she was feeling like she could give Stephanie a run for her money. Not that it mattered, she reminded herself. She was happy Rance had found someone, and she was partially relieved that he had done so first. She probably would have felt guilty if she had been the one to test the waters first.

"Bonjour."

Her breath stalled, but she got it together and smiled at Rance. She got up from her chair and accepted his embrace.

"*Bonjour*," she returned. Damn. He looked good in his suede jacket over a grey sweater and form fitting jeans. She wasn't used to such a fit on a guy before, but Rance pulled it off.

"*Ça va*?" he asked as he took the seat opposite her.

She racked her brain for the little bit of French he had taught her.

"*Ça va*," she replied.

He smiled, pleased, and she relaxed more.

"You look great," he said.

"So do you." She reached for her latte but didn't drink from it. "So, what's up?"

He shook his head. "I don't think I will ever get used to that question. My first reaction is always to reply 'the sky.'"

She chuckled, relieved they could connect in a warm and casual way. "Are you pursuing the remodel of the restaurant you wanted to do?"

"Yes. We're going to redo the entire kitchen and update the dining room."

"That's exciting."

"How about you? Charlene told me you're considering a promotion in Florida."

"You talked to Charlene?"

"I tried you at work the other day. Charlene answered."

"Oh. Well. The promotion's kind of a long shot. Don't really know that I'd want to live in Florida. Charlene thinks it's a bad place for black people."

"Why?"

"I don't know. You know Charlene. She gets these ideas and is convinced they're true. It ain't always roses being black anywhere. I mean, the Bay Area is better that most places, I suppose. But I don't think you called me up to talk about race."

"It didn't seem right not to wish you a Merry Christmas."

She let out a breath. "Yeah. *Joyeux Noël.*"

His eyes seemed to sparkle. "I love it when you speak French."

She smiled, feeling like a bashful girl all of a sudden. "You were a good tutor. You have plans for the holidays?"

"I'm leaving for France in two days to spend Christmas with my family. And you?"

"I'm spending Christmas with my folks, too. In Richmond. It's not as sexy as France, but…"

"It's about family, not geography."

He was staring a little intently at her, so she took a sip of her mildly hot latte.

"I saw a picture of you and Stephanie," she said, not sure if that was the smartest thing to say, but his gaze had unsettled her. Part of her wanted to show him that she was okay with his new path. "She's really cute."

He seemed to stare at her harder.

"Just watch out for your buddy Blaine," she babbled. God, that was stupid. She knew that, as crazy as Blaine was, he wouldn't stoop to hitting on his friend's girlfriend.

At least it seemed to snap Rance out of his stare. "How about you? Have you been…dating?"

"No. Too busy to date."

Bet that sounds familiar, she added silently.

"There's no one…interesting?"

She thought about the drinks she had had with Roy. Roy was easy to talk to, but he had said something in the course of their conversation that he wasn't looking to get on the dating scene yet, partly because he was 'rusty' after being married for over five years. She hadn't been sure if he said that for her benefit or not. In the end, she was just glad that she could connect with someone of the opposite sex without fear or drama.

"Not really," she answered. "I'm working on this RFP for Stanislaus County. They're looking for a financial advisor to oversee all their debts. If I land this client, it could be one of our biggest accounts."

"Good luck."

"Thanks. In fact, I'm meeting with Roger this morning about it."

"I won't keep you, then."

He fished into his coat pocket and pulled out a small box with a green bow. "I got this months ago. Been saving it to give to you for Christmas. Merry Christmas."

He placed it before her. Her heart sank. She hadn't gotten him anything. But most of all, she didn't know what was in the box and what the hell was the right protocol when receiving a gift from one's ex? Trying not to appear too nervous, she loosened the bow and opened the box. She gasped and looked at him.

"They're the ones from Kauai," he confirmed.

"I can't accept these," she blurted, looking down at the shine of the large black pearls surrounded by small sparkling diamonds.

"I bought them for you."

"But…you could give them to…to Steph—"

She started to hand him back the earrings, but he put a hand over hers.

"I want you to have them."

"I don't know. I mean, they're beautiful, but—"

"Wear them in good health."

He got up.

"But I didn't get you anything."

"I don't need anything."

She got up and looked down at the earrings she held. "I don't know what to say. Thank you."

He gave her a hug. "*Tu me manques*."

She tried to remember what that meant. Maybe 'Happy New Year.'

"Merry Christmas, Rance. And Happy New Year," she said after they separated.

He gave her a quick kiss on the cheek and left. She watched him exit the café and heaved a deep sigh.

Sitting back down, she gazed at the gorgeous earrings. Reaching for her latte, she downed the beverage.

"So you're going to the Eve of Erotica, right?"

Audrey, sitting in the Stevenson & Young break room, dipped the tea bag into her mug. She wasn't much of a tea drinker, but if she had another cup of coffee so soon after her latte, her hands would shake too much to get any work done. What she needed was a drink. A glass of burgundy. Or a zinfandel. Thanks to Rance, she actually had some decent bottles of wine at home and had learned to appreciate it. She remembered the very first zinfandel, from the Dry Creek Valley in Sonoma County, that he had had her try on their first day together. She sighed.

"Right?" Charlene pressed as she held and looked at the earrings from Rance.

"What am I supposed to do with these?" Audrey asked.

"Wear them. To the Eve of Erotica."

"A gift from my ex?"

"Honey, it ain't an engagement ring."

"I wish he hadn't given them to me."

"They're gorgeous. I'll take 'em off your hands if you don't want them."

"No, that don't feel right."

"So, what, you gonna keep them but never wear 'em? That don't make sense."

Audrey sipped her tea, then grimaced. She had left the tea bag in too long.

Charlene looked more closely at the earrings. "These must be expensive."

"That's why I didn't buy them myself. Honestly, who needs to wear thousands of dollars worth of jewelry?"

"But if you can, why not? It's not like Rance broke the bank getting these."

"And I'm supposed to be more impressed because he's got money to spare? Like he can buy my affection?"

Charlene gave her a knowing look. "You know Rance isn't like that. You *should* be impressed because he wanted to surprise you, and he gave you the earrings even though you aren't his damn girlfriend anymore. Be grateful, honey."

Audrey took the earrings back. "These earrings could buy a lot of meals for a lot of families."

"So can my Prada bag, though I got it at the outlet mall. Stop guilt tripping yourself. And Rance. He's not like most rich dudes."

Audrey had to admit Charlene was right. Rance was more than charitable, and despite being a businessman, he was almost a socialist in his politics. The *Hotel Sur Mer* paid the highest wages of any hotel in the City, and he always had loyal, quality employees as a result.

"Of course it cuts into profits," he had said when she had asked him about it before. "But running a business isn't just about making as much money as you can or making more money than the next guy."

"It is in America," she had quipped.

"At least in America you have the freedom to run a business the way that you see fit, for better or worse. It isn't as easy in other countries."

Audrey got up and dumped her tea down the sink and started over with a new cup.

"So, the Eve of Erotica," Charlene said. "I have some ideas for a costume I think would look smokin' on you."

"I haven't been in a costume since I last went trick-or-treating."

"You'll love it. It's just as much fun. Besides...your mystery guy will be there."

Audrey started. Her pulse skipped a beat. "How do you know?"

"Trey has the guest list. He said all but a handful of people from the Naughty Noel can't make it. And the ones who can't make it are spoken for or not the right orientation."

"Doesn't mean the guy from the Naughty Noel will show. And even if he did, it doesn't mean he'd be interested in doing anything with me again."

"But you'd want to if he did?" Charlene pounced.

"I'm not sure."

"What's holding you back?"

"Roy said he'd be back out here the second week of January."

"You said he said that he wasn't ready to hit the dating scene again."

"I know. But he's a normal, decent guy. I like that."

"What? And Rance isn't normal or decent?"

"What does Rance have to do with it?"

"Nothing. I mean, it's just—you can be a decent person but have a wild, kinky side. You do."

Audrey smiled. "Yeah, I guess I do."

"Going to the Eve of Erotica isn't going to ruin your chances with Roy if and when he wants to date again. And I don't want to go the Eve of Erotica alone. I'll even help you at the soup kitchen next weekend."

"Damn, girl, you're keen on me going."

Charlene put more marshmallows in her hot chocolate. "I just have this hunch you're gonna like it."

9

Once a naval base, Treasure Island was now home to over six thousand civilians, office buildings, hangars that were used as film and sound stages, and wineries. Many of the old naval barracks were now townhouses, and Chris's family had purchased a number of them to use for their porn film business.

By the time Blaine arrived, the party was already in full swing. The main gallery, a former barracks hold, was awash in red lighting. Music pulsed off the walls. Scantily-clad servers carried trays of gelatin shots. Despite the cold temperature outside, it was *hot* inside. In the back of the room, a stage had been set up for erotic demonstrations. At the moment three strippers dressed in CHP outfits were dancing. Blaine had considered a law enforcement outfit of some type, but had settled on something more unique, though it wasn't perhaps the most practical attire if things got hot and heavy. The powdered wig he had on was beginning to itch, and the thing called a cravat around his neck was too warm. He also had on breeches, stockings, buckled heels, a waistcoat, and tailcoat.

He brushed past two half-naked women kissing and a table where Madge the Midget, a local porn star, was signing autographs. He stopped to admire a body art painter brushing the spots of a cheetah on a completely naked woman. Turning around, he bumped into a petite French maid.

"Blaine?"

He surveyed the brunette in thigh-high stockings and an outfit with apron that barely covered her underwear—if she was wearing underwear.

"Samantha?" he replied, recognizing the young woman he had dated briefly. Barely over twenty-one, she had proved too young at the time. They hadn't lasted long.

"I guess I'm not surprised to see you here," she said with a small laugh.

He couldn't say the same about her, though he couldn't remember much about her except that she spent a lot of time lounging beside the pool at the country club.

"You're looking good. Sexy," he said with a friendly smile.

She giggled. "It's my first time here."

"You'll have fun. There's some extreme stuff here, though."

"And weird. I passed by an area that was designated for Cyborg Sex?"

"Anything goes. Who are you here with?"

"Two of my friends, former sorority sisters of mine."

He noticed the drink in her hand. "Just watch the alcohol consumption, especially since it's your first time."

"I will... You're sweet when you're protective like that."

He didn't say anything. He wasn't looking to reconnect with Samantha, but he could tell she was interested.

"I'm looking for a friend, but it was good to see you."

She smiled though disappointment filled her eyes. "Good to see you, too, Blaine."

He gave her a hug then continued on his way. Six steps later, he heard a voice behind him.

"Wow. I didn't figure you for a jailbait fisher."

Recognizing the voice, he turned around. His jaw hit the floor. There would be a lot of boners at tonight's party thanks to Cleopatra-Charlene. She had on a kind of bikini halter made from sheer white material and a gold band. Then there was nothing but her beautiful naked torso—his favorite part of a woman was that area from her ribcage to the navel and swell of the hips—until the golden jeweled belt that circled just below her hip bone and from which hung the same sheer white fabric. Two large slits in the skirts showed off her legs. She had on some other items: golden sandals, a beaded headdress, and a bracelet on her upper arm.

Shit, I can't believe I promised to stop trying to score with her.

"You'll get yourself arrested for child molestation," she added.

"Samantha looks younger than she is," he replied, still mesmerized by what had to be the sexiest thing he had ever seen.

"Right." Charlene looked him over. "So who or what are you supposed to be? George Washington?"

"The Marquis de Sade," he replied.

"Who now?"

"He's the 'S' in BDSM."

"Oh."

He looked around. "Where's Audrey?"

"She's here."

"No deal till I see for myself."

She looked in the direction of where Audrey stood watching a large screen above head showing Nagisa Oshima's *In the Realm of the Senses*. Audrey was wearing a backless leather halter dress, thigh-high boots, and a mask over her eyes.

"That's Audrey?" Blaine asked.

"I got her to the party. What happens from here isn't part of the deal."

He nodded and from his coat pocket pulled out the gift certificate. "Worth twelve meals at Ballander's."

He handed it to her. She looked at it almost as if she didn't believe it.

"There's no value listed. Should I keep the bill under a certain amount?"

"It'll be charged to my account. Just don't go crazy."

She looked at him, maybe feeling a little guilty about her prize. "Wow. Thanks. This is...worth a lot."

"Don't sweat it. The hard part is not being able to hit on you anymore."

And he looked her over again for emphasis. He bet if the lighting was brighter, he could see her nipples through the fabric.

She smiled. "You make a pretty sexy George Washington yourself."

"I'm gonna find Rance and let him know Audrey's here. If I stay here looking at you much longer, I won't be able to keep up my end of the deal."

It was true. He felt like his balls were going to bust. He didn't even dare give her a good-bye hug.

"*Au revoir, mademoiselle*," he said with a smile and gallant bow.

She seemed surprised by his departure, as if she didn't believe he could make it without attempting to hit on her at least once.

"You owe me, Durand," Blaine said to Rance.

Rance was dressed in a Zorro outfit with most of his face wrapped in black. Blaine had tried to talk him out of the costume. While Zorro could be a sexy hero, there wasn't anything inherently *erotic* in the dude.

He looked back through the crowd and saw a big beefy guy with tattoos all over his arms try to hit on Charlene.

"Is Audrey here?" Rance asked.

"Yeah. She's in a black leather dress and eye mask watching the big screen TV right now."

"Thanks."

Blaine watched Rance head in Audrey's direction and thought about getting himself a stiff drink. For the first time ever, he wished he hadn't come to the Eve of Erotica.

"That's unsimulated sex," the man next to Audrey said.

"Hunh?" Audrey replied as she watched Sada strangle Ishida as they made love.

"Unsimulated sex," the guy repeated. "Means the actors were really having sex, not just pretending."

She looked at the short and scrawny man wearing nothing but handprints and decided the movie was much more attractive.

"Sure. That's what porn is."

"*In the Realm of the Senses* is not porn," he said as if she had insulted him. "It's a classic art-film by Nagisa Oshima, released in 1976. This is an awful version because of the dubbing. Subtitles are much better."

Audrey studied the screen. The movie did seem to have a story to it beyond the cheesy settings of most porns.

"For you, madam," a cocktail server wearing a corset and thigh-high nylons said as she presented Audrey with a note. "Drink?"

"Pass," Audrey replied as she took the note. She opened it and her breath caught as she read it:

Eleven o'clock. Unit 3765.

Your friend from the Naughty Noel.

Her pulse quickened. She turned to the man beside her.

"You got the time?"

"Do I look like I have a watch on me?" he replied, then muttered something in Japanese in sync with Sada.

Looking around, Audrey saw Charlene and went to her friend.

"What's wrong? You look lost," Audrey said.

"He meant it," Charlene replied, looking down at a slip of paper.

Audrey looked over Charlene's shoulders. "Ballander's! How'd you get that?"

"It's from Blaine. He's, like, a co-owner."

"The guy must want to lay you bad, girl."

"Not as bad as I thought."

"You crazy? A man does not hand out gift certificates to Ballander's without expecting something in return."

"Actually, he promised me he wouldn't hit on me again." Charlene spoke as if from far away.

"Are we talking about Blaine Edwards? Sandy hair? Friend of Rance?"

"Yeah."

"Don't believe him."

"But I do. He just walked off."

"Probably playing hard to get."

"Not even a hug good-bye."

Audrey stared at Charlene in disbelief. She knew her friend didn't do drugs, but maybe Charlene had inhaled some pot walking around.

"If I were you, I'd give the certificate back, just in case."

That seemed to snap Charlene out of her trance. "Are you shittin' me? A gift certificate to Ballander's?!"

She folded the gift certificate into a tiny square and tucked it in the band at her hip. "So, what's up with you?"

"It's him," she replied, handing Charlene the note.

"You gonna do it?" Charlene asked after reading it and handing it back.

"I don't know."

"Sure you are. You didn't come all this way and get dressed up for nothing."

Audrey took a deep breath. She was supposed it was true.

Charlene took her by the arm. "C'mon, let's get you a drink."

"I thought you recommend not drinking at these things. I mean, just because it went okay the first time doesn't mean he won't get psycho on me. In fact, I'm surprised I didn't think about that before."

"No, no, no! He won't. You can trust him."

"How do you know?"

Charlene had a bewildered look, like a child who had been caught doing something they weren't supposed to.

Audrey's eyes widened. "You set this up!"

"I didn't! I swear! I—I just know the guy. He's good."

"I can't believe you! Who is he?"

"A friend of...Trey's. So, if there's a problem, I'll let Trey know. He'll beat the shit out of the guy."

"What's the guy's name?"

"Look, if I tell you, it'll take the fun out of it. So just, go with it. Have fun. It's just for one night. You don't ever have to see him again after tonight."

"Does he know who I am?"

"I don't know. He doesn't care."

"What if he takes my photo and posts it on his Facebook account?"

"He doesn't have a Facebook account."

"How do you know?"

"I looked before. Just...trust me."

Audrey stared at her friend as if she could glean the truth if she stared hard enough. She didn't quite trust Charlene, but there was an earnestness to her voice that was unusual.

"You realize if something goes wrong, our friendship is in jeopardy," Audrey tested.

"Yeah, yeah, now let's get that drink and find out what time it is."

Reluctantly, Audrey allowed herself to be led to the bar. She did need a little liquid courage.

"What do you say I conquer you tonight?"

Charlene looked up from her rum and Coke at a Roman gladiator complete with sandals and helmet. He had rubbed something on onto his body because his chest gleamed. She surveyed his muscular limbs. He had a tasty looking body. Face wasn't bad. But for some strange reason, she wasn't that interested.

"Maybe another time, Caesar," she replied.

He leaned against the bar near her anyway. "You know it was Marc Anthony, not Caesar, that was Cleopatra's lover."

Smart ass, she thought to herself, though she felt the absence of a college education. It wasn't the first time she was a little self-conscious about it. She was smart enough for college. Audrey used to encourage her to go back and get her bachelor's, but she didn't like studying. It was too passive for her. And giving up the steady income from a job to rack up student loans hadn't appealed to her either.

"Didn't know I had to have a history degree for this party," she retorted.

"I can teach you all you need to know."

She hopped off her stool and stared at his pecs. They were nice pecs. "I'll think about it."

"Can I at least get your name? A number?"

"Name's Cleopatra. And I don't give out my number at these things."

"I can rock your world," he called after her as she walked into the crowd with her drink.

She found a balcony outside and stood beside a heater lamp to drink in relative peace. In the corner of the balcony, a dyke was hitting on a petite blonde wearing a merrywidow. Charlene looked into her glass. It was her second drink. She hadn't eaten much so she shouldn't finish it. She looked at the row of townhouses across the lawn. They used to house the families of military personnel. Chris's husband used them for scenes in his porn flicks. Rance and Audrey would be in one of those units. Probably getting it on. She felt a little jealous. It wouldn't be so bad if she had someone like Rance in her life. She might be inspired to be a good girl.

Or not. She wasn't ready to settle down or anything like that. Right now, she just wanted to get laid. She wanted to be in the middle of a good fuck session when the clock struck midnight. She couldn't think of a better way to ring in the new year than with an orgasm. Maybe she should go back to that Roman dude.

"So the unit at the far end is the one with S and M stuff," a woman below was saying.

"Yeah?"

Charlene started. She recognized the second voice. It was Blaine. She took another sip of her drink, wondering if she should stay, but she far too curious.

"You ever been in gang bang?" a woman asked.

"As part of the gang or the one getting banged?" replied Blaine.

"Either."

"No and no. Not sure I'd be into the first. But if you're talking me and a half dozen babes, I'd be up for that."

Charlene shook her head. Of course he would. She took a larger sip.

"Ever been tied up?" asked the woman.

"A few times."

"Been with more than one girl?"

"A few times."

Of course, Charlene thought to herself with another gulp.

"What do you like best about it?"

"All of it. I like it when they put on a show for me. I like it when I've got one riding my face while the other one rides my cock."

Charlene finished her drink at the vision of two women with Blaine.

"You're too scrumptious. I promised my gal pals that I'd share whatever I find."

"How many friends are there?"

"Three others. You think you can handle all of us?"

"I think we'd have a fun time trying."

"Why don't you wait at the end unit? Give me, like, twenty minutes to round up the gang."

"I'll get us a cozy room for five."

Charlene heard the clicking of high heels as the woman walked away. Blaine with four women. He couldn't fuck them all at once. She wondered if he could last long enough to fuck them all in turn. What would a man do with four women? She stared into her now-empty glass. Shit. She was going to be more buzzed than she wanted to be. But then she had an idea. She looked across at the townhouses and figured out which one was the far end unit.

10

Rance drew in a deep breath. He surveyed the bedroom with satisfaction. He had tried to make it look as romantic as possible. Dozens of red candles flickered in the darkness. He had changed out the bed sheets and replaced them with higher quality sheets made of Egyptian cotton, with a thread count of 1,000. On a bedside table, he had placed a bottle of champagne, glasses, and light almond cookies. He sat down on an armchair opposite the bed. He felt as nervous, maybe more nervous, than his first day impersonating a gigolo. Somehow, it felt like there was more at stake here. What if she managed to figure out his identity? Would she be offended? Would she think he was a crazy pervert? He rubbed his temples and wished he hadn't opted for the Zorro costume. It was hard breathing through the mask. He decided to get on his feet again.

"Hola."

He whipped around. Audrey stood in the doorway. He recognized her form and those voluptuous lips. The most voluptuous lips he had ever known. *Mon Dieu.* How he missed kissing them. Stephanie had full lips, but they didn't feel as tender beneath his own. Maybe it was because she had gone through a lip augmentation. In any case, they didn't compare to the lips Audrey had naturally. She looked stunning, too, in her outfit. Those thigh-high boots encasing supple legs made the blood course to his groin.

"*Hola, senorita,*" he replied with his best attempt at a Spanish accent.

He had prepared a few Spanish phrases for this evening. But he might have been better off dressing as Leopold von Sacher-Masoch since his German was flawless. Despite all his time working and living in California, he knew very little Spanish. Even his Japanese was better than his Spanish.

He made a gesture for her to come in. She took in the ambiance as she entered. He discerned her approval and relaxed a little.

"*Champan?*" he queried.

"I suppose a glass won't hurt."

The Spanish was working. She didn't seem to recognize his voice. He easily popped the cork on the bottle of Krug Clos du Mesnil. The champagne might have given him away, but Audrey wasn't that familiar with the label. She had known next to nothing about wines in general prior to their relationship. He had enjoyed teaching her how to taste and appreciate wine. One of his favorite outings had been driving her up to Sonoma County and giving her a brief oenology lesson.

She was a quick study, but they had not gotten to sparkling wines. He handed her a glass.

"You're not having any?" she asked, studying the glass with suspicion. "You didn't slip a roofie in here or nothing'?"

"Que?"

What was a 'roofie'? he wondered. Was it that date-rape drug?

"Nevermind. I guess you don't really need to resort to that. You're getting some action either way. Unless you're a necrophiliac. You're not a necrophiliac, are you?"

He shook his head and hands. She was—what was the word?—babbling. She was nervous. He poured himself a glass and gestured that he would drink, too.

"*¡Salud!*" he said, lifting his glass.

Peeling the mask to uncover his mouth, he drank the champagne. Reassured, she took a sip. Then another.

"Wow. This is really good."

She finished her glass.

"Mas?"

"Just a little," she replied. "The bubbles go to my head quick."

He poured her more, then set the bottle on the table. She sat down on the bed and crossed her legs. He gazed at her boots once more. She had worn boots on their first "date," though they were nothing like the ones she had on now.

"So, what's with the Spanish tonight?"

"*Soy Zorro,*" he replied with a sweeping bow.

"Un-hunh. Zorro never really factored into my fantasies, but I guess I can dig it." She gave him an appraising sweep of the eyes. "You look anything like Antonio Banderas?"

Remembering that she had once been disappointed to find he looked nothing like Denzel Washington, he replied, *"Si tu veux—quieres."*

He held his breath for a second, but she did not catch the slip in French. She finished her champagne.

"So...you're a friend of Trey's?" she asked.

He wondered who or how she had come to that conclusion. He gestured "sort of."

"You do this anonymous lover thing with a lot of women?"

Que toi, he wanted to respond. What was the Spanish version? *Que tu? Solemente usted? Solo usted?* He decided to just shake his head.

She ran her hand over the bed sheet. "Dang. This is nice. It's almost as nice as what they got at fancy hotels. Like the *Hotel sur Mer."*

His throat tightened. *"Sí, es bueno."*

"You gonna do this Zorro thing all night long?"

He nodded.

"Well, my Spanish is limited. Outside of ordering lunch in the South Mission, I haven't used Spanish since taking it in high school."

Her Spanish was still better than his. He kept quiet and approached her. The less talking, the better.

"But I'm guessing we won't need to do that much talking," she said, her voice catching, as he ran a gloved hand down her bare arm.

He couldn't believe he was doing this. But how could he pass up an opportunity to be with her? Somewhere in the back of his mind, he wondered if he was being fair to her. He knew who she was, but she didn't know who he was. The nagging thought faded, however, when he traced her bottom lip with his thumb. He wanted to kiss her, badly, but he needed to keep the mask on for now.

"Muy hermosa."

Her breath deepened. "*Mercí.* I mean, *gracias.*"

He smiled to himself at her slip. In French, no less.

"But you don't have to keep up the Zorro act. I'm not one of those women who melt just 'cause a guy has an accent."

Yes, he knew that. In college, women had swooned left and right at his French. He hadn't come across a woman as unaffected as Audrey.

He reached for her mask but she put a quick hand to his to stop him.

"Are you removing yours?" she asked.

He shook his head.

"But you want me to take off mine?"

Stepping back, he went to a dresser and picked up a satin red blindfold. Returning, he held it out for her to see.

"I take it that's for me," she noted. She took a deep breath. "Okay. Charlene says I can trust you, though why *I* trust *Charlene* is suspect. Can I trust you?"

The stare she pinned on him was unnerving. He was tempted to reveal himself, give her the truth. She deserved it, didn't she? If she knew who he was, she probably wouldn't want to go through with this. Was he only serving his own selfish desires by seeing this through? But she was interested in sex, too. She wouldn't be here if she wasn't. Did he really want to ruin her erotic tryst with a stranger and make the night hellishly awkward?

He nodded in response.

"Okay, I'm ready. Sort of. I'm ready. Really."

He stroked her cheek. Dear, charming Audrey. She had a wild, adventurous streak, but she suppressed it with too much thinking. This time he waited for her to remove her mask. She did so swiftly, as if it were a band-aid that would hurt less with a quick yank. He wrapped the satin cloth across her eyes and tied it securely behind her head.

"Shit!" Charlene swore as she caught her sandal on the uneven pavement leading up to Unit 3737. She shouldn't have finished off that second rum and Coke so quickly.

Pushing open the door, she stepped into the foyer. It was dark except for the votives along the walls. She vaguely discerned a slender young man tied to a cross in the living room. There was a sharp crack, and the young man wailed. She saw the back of a man wearing a black hood and tight black pants, holding a flogger. Aware of her presence, he turned.

"You looking for a go, Cleo?" he asked her.

"Any private rooms in here?" she asked.

"Upstairs."

"Thanks."

Holding onto the rail, she headed up the stairs. It was one of the larger townhomes with three bedrooms. One of them was already occupied. She could tell by the rutting sounds coming from behind the closed doors. The smaller room didn't have a bed. It had stockades and a pommel. She couldn't see how this room lent itself to a five-some. She headed into the master bedroom next.

Bingo.

This room had a queen bed with shackles dangling from each of the four bedposts. The bed was bare except for a white fitted cotton sheet. Though there were a few votives scattered throughout the room, most of the lighting came from the moon outside. There were implements hanging from the walls: mostly whips, paddles, crops, and canes. She stood before one wall and removed a folded leather belt. She smacked it lightly on her palm and wondered what it would feel like against her ass.

"Charlene?"

Whipping around, she saw Blaine standing in the doorway. Her heart skipped a beat. He didn't seem particularly happy to see her. Probably because he was anticipating his rendezvous with the four *gal pals*.

"You got this room?" he asked.

"No," she answered. "I just—I heard about the room and wanted to check it out."

"Oh."

She fingered the leather belt. "You ever use one of these?"

She tried to play it off like the thing amused her, but she wasn't sure she was successful.

"No."

It was hard to tell through the dim lighting and the haze of her intoxication, but it seemed the pupils of his eyes had dilated.

"Ever spank someone?" she asked.

"Yes."

Damn. She wanted to ask him if he'd spank her. He leaned against the doorframe and crossed his arms.

"What happened to Julius Caesar?" he asked.

"Marc Anthony," she corrected. "Caesar didn't get it on with Cleopatra."

"Not true. Caesar and Cleopatra had a son together."

Her lower lip dropped. "I thought so! 'Cause I kinda remember seeing that Liz Taylor movie when I was young and thinking, damn, she's gettin' with a man old enough to be her grandfather."

"So are you expecting Marc Anthony here?"

She replaced the leather belt. "Nah. He wanted to give me a lesson on Roman history. I hated history."

Blaine finally smiled.

"I mean, I might have liked it, but my high school history teacher ruined it for me. He was always staring at my tits and asking if I wanted some after-school tutoring."

"Gross."

"Yeah."

She went to the bed and felt the sheet. It was dry and didn't seem to have any spots. She sat down. "Don't think this bed's been used yet."

She lay down and stretched. Blaine stiffened immediately. She stared up at the shackles. Part of her couldn't believe she was doing this, but the alcohol was suppressing any better judgment.

"You ever been tied up before?" she asked.

"Yeah....You?"

She nodded. "But not with shackles. These are made of iron and shit."

"The leather ones are below."

She lowered her gaze and saw them resting at the bottom of the posts. They were connected to some harness beneath the bed. A warm sensation began spreading through her loins.

"Put one on me."

The words were out of her mouth before she could stop them. His eyes widened.

"I just wanna see what it feels like."

He only frowned. "Look, I'm expecting—"

"Just do it. It's not going to take long."

He had a hard set to his jaw. "You're drunk."

"I'm buzzed, not drunk."

"I thought you didn't get drunk at these events."

"I thought you were Mr. Sadism. Nevermind. I'll do it myself."

Blaine peeled himself off the doorframe and approached the bed. He took one of the restraints and cinched it around her wrist in one quick motion. It was a little snug but not too uncomfortable.

"Wow. It's like you've done this before," she said. "Now do the other one."

He hesitated but knelt on the bed and reached over her for the other cuff. She stared up at his waistcoat. It was a lot of fucking clothes to take off. And yet, it was kind of sexy. His body hovering over her was making her crazy. She wanted him. There was no denying it. She didn't know why, and why now, but she didn't care. She'd figure it out some other time. For now, she was going to find a way to fuck Blaine Edwards.

Fuck me, Blaine cursed himself as he glanced down at Charlene. Bad move. The sight of her made the blood rush to his groin. She was tethered to the bed beneath him. How the fuck had that happened? He made a move to get off the bed, but she bent her leg and it grazed the inside of his thigh. He quickly clamped down on her thigh to keep her from touching his now-hardened cock. The feel of her naked skin against his hand made him ten degrees hotter.

"What are you doing?" he asked, more harshly than he intended.

She stared at him with glassy eyes. And then he saw it. Her arousal. He had been with too many women not to recognize it, see it, smell it, sense it. He was sure of it. What he didn't know was how much of it was the alcohol. She arched her back, and her breasts nearly grazed him. Was she trying to seduce him? This was crazy. He had promised he wouldn't hit on her anymore. It was what she wanted, right?

"You ever get into any BDSM shit?" she asked.

He needed to get away from her. Untie her and send her on her way. But his body wouldn't budge. As if he were some moth drawn to a flame. Drawn to the heat of her body. But unlike the moth, he knew he was going to get burned.

"I read *Fifty Shades*," he answered.

"You read Fifty Shades?"

"It's pretty tame."

"Yeah? You know from experience?"

"I've been to a few events at the Citadel before."

Her brows went up. "Really? The one, uh, near Eddy Street?"

"It's on Eddy Street. You've never been there?"

He was a little surprised that, with Charlene's openness to all things sexual, she hadn't tried the BDSM club yet.

"I've been curious, but I haven't found the right partner to go with."

"You don't need a partner."

She seemed to be considering the prospect.

"I'm kind of expecting...people," he told her, half wishing that wasn't the case. He should sit upright and not hover over her. The proximity of her body was doing something to the air between them. If he touched her, there was no going back.

"So lock the door."

What?! He stared at her. She had spoken so softly, he wasn't sure he had heard her correctly. The smoldering look she was giving him should have been sufficient corroboration, but he still couldn't believe it.

"Lock the door," she repeated.

He suddenly felt annoyed. What kind of stunt was she pulling? Did she get off on teasing him? Was she on some power trip because she knew he'd give just about anything to bury his cock inside of her right now?

"Charlene, I got four ladies coming to blow my mind—and other parts, hopefully—and I promised I wasn't going to hit on you anymore."

"You didn't promise not to fuck me."

This time he got off the bed. His mind spun. His cock throbbed. "What?"

"Look, I'm tied to the bed. I'm sexy. I'm horny."

"You're drunk."

"Maybe. But I want to get laid."

"I'm sure more than half the people here would lay you. Like that Marc Anthony dude."

She glared at him. "Will you stop being such an asshole and fuck me?"

He stomped over to the door and turned the lock. This was some kind of test. Women were always thinking up ways to test a guy.

"Finally!" she praised. "What does a girl have to do to get laid around here?"

He watched her writhe against her restraints. Damn. She was so sexy. So fucking sexy. Had he really promised he wouldn't hit on her again? Was he crazy?

She looked over at him. "What's the matter? You don't want a piece of Cleopatra?"

A muscle along his jaw tightened. His cock stretched painfully against his pants.

"You're gonna wake up tomorrow regretting what happened, and then you're gonna be pissed at me for it," he replied.

"I'm a grown woman. I don't regret these sorts of things. As for being pissed, yeah, I'm pissed. Right now. 'Cause you ain't doin' a damn thing!"

He pressed his lips together grimly. He didn't want to take advantage of her intoxicated state, but, on the other hand, he was only human. A male human at that. A yard away from the hottest woman at the party.

Dozens of men and women would have loved to have a go at her body. Was he really going to be lucky bastard that got her?

She bent her legs. The fabric of her costume fell around and between them. She had luscious legs. Creamy, milk chocolate legs. He imagined them wrapped about his hips as he plunged into her. Deep.

"What's the matter, Edwards? You forget how to fuck or something?"

He walked back to the bed and eyed her keenly. Was it possible that she wanted a fucking, not just from anyone, but from him? The sensation at his groin surged at the thought.

He crossed his arms. "Had a change of heart, hunh? Decided you want me after all."

She frowned, then pursed her lips. "Yeah, you'll do."

"Oh no. You want me to fuck you, you aren't getting off that easy."

She furrowed her brow, perplexed. He sat down on the bed beside her and lightly ran his knuckles along her exposed leg. Her breath hitched.

"What do you mean?" she demanded.

"You gotta admit it."

"Admit what?"

"That you want the Blaine-ster."

She rolled her eyes. He reached down and applied a restraint to her ankle. She gasped.

"So tell me, what about BDSM intrigues you?"

"I dunno. Everything."

"Would you like being a dominatrix? Or a sex slave?"

She inhaled sharply. "I don't know about the slave part, but I like my men on the alpha side. Dominating.

There's something cool about surrendering control, I suppose. A little scary, but sexy at the same time."

He restrained her other ankle. The bonds were loose enough to allow her some movement. She wasn't pulled taut to all four corners and could still keep her knees bent. He thought about pulling the restraints tighter. The thought of her spread eagle just about killed him.

"You like that?" he asked, surveying her. His blood was pounding.

She licked her lips and wriggled a little. "Yeah."

"You look super hot tied up," he said, doubting he could hold back for much longer. He was ready to attack her.

She grinned. "I know."

He passed a hand over her belly. She had a cute belly button.

"You game for more than just being tied up?"

She followed his gaze to the implements on the wall. "Maybe."

He slid his hand beneath the curve of her buttock. "Your ass does beg to be walloped."

She groaned, and he wondered how wet she had gotten. He sunk his fingers into her butt cheek. God, the things he wanted to do with her ass...

"It is such a fine piece of ass."

"So fuck it already."

"You haven't admitted you want me yet."

She huffed in exasperation.

"Indulge my narcissism." He slid his hand to the inside of her thigh. "It's easy. All you have to say is, 'I want Blaine Edwards to fuck me.'"

He caressed the length of her thigh.

"You're such a dick."

He gave her thigh a sharp but playful slap. "Go on. You can do it: I want Blaine Edwards to fuck me."

He slipped his hand to her crotch and rubbed her through the fabric. From the way the cloth slid against her, he guessed her to be very, very wet. Moaning, she tried to grind herself harder into his hand.

He urged her, "'I want Blaine Edwards to fuck me.'"

She relented. "I want Blaine Edwards to fuck me."

He rewarded her by fondling her more. Brushing aside the costume, he found her g-string. He slid his fingers under the tiny bit of fabric. Yep, she was wet all right. He teased her clit, loving the soft lilting grunts his caress elicited from her. The tension at his own crotch mounted, but he held off.

"Say it again," he instructed.

"I want...I want..."

He was thumbing her clit, coating the bud with the juices from below. His head swam like never before. She had such a sweet pussy. But he had an inspiration, and he wasn't going to let the opportunity pass him by.

"Let's say it together: I want Blaine Edwards to fuck me."

He agitated his hand against her till she squirmed.

"I want...ohhhh...I want Blaine Edwards...oh...to fuck me!"

"Long and hard."

"Long and hard!"

"Nice."

He inserted two of his fingers into her wetness and had to close his eyes at how hot she felt. Her pussy was like a furnace. A hot, wet furnace. He rubbed his fingers in the area behind her clitoris while keeping his thumb where it was. She bowed off the bed.

"Oh my God! Oh my God!" she cried.

He increased the vigor of his ministrations. Her fingers curled tight. She tugged against the restraints. Grunting. Groaning. Writhing. It was a beautiful sight.

"Yes! Right there! Yes!" she screamed.

But he slowed his pace. He leaned toward her ear and whispered, "Say it again. I love hearing you say how much you want me to fuck you."

"I want Blaine Edwards to fuck me long and hard!"

He stroked her G-spot till she didn't know whether to pant or groan or cry. It was now or never.

"And I want to be his sex slave for a week."

At first it didn't seem like she heard. Or maybe she was deliberately ignoring him. So he slowed his caress until his fingers barely moved.

"Say it," he encouraged.

She opened her eyes and stared at him. He had the feeling that if she wasn't restrained, she'd be busting his balls.

"What?" she asked.

He wasn't the kind of guy who liked to beat about the bush, whether it was in the boardroom or in the bedroom. In meetings, he often started off stating what he wanted, followed with, "Now how we do make it happen?" He always liked shifting the conversation away from the "what" question to the "how" question. And in the course of his successful business ventures, he was never once nervous about putting out a proposition.

But this was different. He was aiming high—higher than he had ever aimed because he didn't know Charlene all that well. And until a few minutes ago, he hadn't even been all that sure that she liked him. She had tolerated him because he was Rance's friend, and he was sure her ego liked his attentions, but being his sex slave for a week...he wasn't sure he'd agree to it if he were her. He circled her clit as an enticement. She made a low, guttural purr.

"Be my sex slave for a week," he restated, and locked gazes with her so that she knew he meant business.

"You gotta be shittin' me, white boy."

"Race doesn't have anything to do with it."

"A white guy wants a black woman to be his slave. How is that not fucked up?"

"It's just a fucking coincidence that I'm white and you're—Look, it's about sex. Just sex. You like it. I like it. You said you were curious to try out some BDSM. Here's your chance."

She narrowed her eyes at him. He started hitting her G-spot again.

"I promise you'll like it," he assured.

She whimpered.

"I'll even throw in another year's worth of dining at Ballander's."

"For me and a guy?"

"You can bring your boyfriend's boyfriend."

He couldn't tell if she was considering the proposition or just fixated on his stroking her. The knocking at the door jarred them both. He could hear three or four women giggling from the other side.

"Mr. de Sade, are you in there?" one of them asked.

Ignoring them, he continued to stare at Charlene. "Well?"

She shook her head a little, resisting.

"I won't do anything to you that you don't want me to," he promised.

"Ain't it enough I'm gonna let you fuck me right now?"

"What can I say, I'm a greedy bastard. It's worked for me in business."

"Mr. de Sade!" called the woman who had approached him first. "Your gang bang is here."

"You're scared," he said to Charlene.

"Of you, white boy?" she spat.

The "white boy" thing was irritating, but he didn't say anything. Instead, he fondled her faster. "You're scared I'm gonna fuck you so good, you're gonna want to be my sex slave permanently."

She groaned. There was a pounding at the door.

"Maybe he's not in there," one of them said. "Maybe someone else's got the room."

"Hurry up in there!" another yelled.

The pounding intensified.

"Should I let them in?" he asked Charlene.

Her eyes widened. The thought of the four women ravishing Charlene was too much.

"Well? What's it going to be?" he pressed.

"If I say 'no'?" she asked, her voice uncertain.

"You can get your fucking, but it'll be from the four horny women out there."

God, he was going to hell. He meant it jokingly. But from the frown on her face, he could tell she thought he was serious.

"That's blackmail," she accused.

"I want what I want."

"No way. You've been wanting to fuck me since the day you laid eyes on me. You ain't passing this up."

"True. But I am going to get off good watching four women go to town on your hot bod."

There was now more than one woman pounding on the door. Charlene looked at him, a little alarmed. He said nothing, awaiting her answer patiently. It was the most excruciating thing he had ever done.

"Fine!"

He barely heard her above the noise at the door. "Fine, what?"

"I'll be your sex slave for a week!"

Holy shit. He had just gotten the Christmas gift of a lifetime.

11

Charlene didn't have time to process what she had just agreed to. His fingers pumped vehemently into her, the heel of his palm striking her clit. Despite the alcohol in her system, she quickly came, the muscles of her pussy spasming around his fingers as her body twitched and jerked against the restraints. His fingers coaxed wave after wave of ecstasy. The pounding at the door had become one with her rapid heartbeat. And she almost didn't care if the women on the other side broke the door down. All that mattered was that she was feeling *good...really, really good.*

Her cry had been heard on the other side--one of the women said, "I told you someone else was in there."

"Hey, I wanna come, too!" another giggled.

Blaine eased his fingers out of her and rubbed her mound, gently eking out the last shivers from her orgasm. She stared at the ceiling as she basked in the afterglow of her climax, feeling warm and satiated. A part of her was still aroused, and if he kept touching her, she'd soon want to come again.

He read her mind. "Don't worry, you'll get another."

She relaxed into the restraints.

"You think the guy bailed on us?" one of the women outside asked.

"His loss," replied another. "Let's go make out in that smaller room there."

There was a scuffling sound around the door, then silence. Charlene stared at Blaine. She still wanted him to fuck her. But what was it she had agreed to?

"Should I have invited them in?" he asked with a lazy smile.

"No!"

"Don't tell me The Hot One has never been with another woman?"

"I've done it a couple times," she answered candidly and was gratified to see his eyes widen. "But I don't know these women from Adam."

"Isn't that part of the fun?"

"Yeah, but I don't know what they look like—what if they're a bunch of nasty-looking hoes with smelly twats? I don't go for just any pussy, you know."

"What if they were good-looking babes with pussy as sweet as yours?"

He fingered her folds and she shivered again.

"Maybe," she replied.

"Shit," he exhaled, his gaze burning.

Men, she smiled to herself. Women making out with women got them so ridiculously turned on.

He got off the bed to take off his eighteenth-century coat. She had to hand it to him. He had more self-control than she would have thought. Given the way he had looked at her, she thought for sure he was going to launch himself at her.

"Would you really have let those women in?" she asked, watching him as he slowly unbuttoned his waistcoat. She had seen him once at the gym of that pricey club he and Rance belonged to. Blaine had a good physique, a little more muscular where Rance was lean. She supposed, for a white guy, Blaine was pretty yummy.

"Only if you had agreed to it," he replied.

"You mean you were just bullshittin' when you said I could get fucked by four horny women?"

"Blackmail's not my thing. Never really needed to resort to it before."

"But—"

She glared at him. He peeled off the waistcoat.

"Hey, I can't help it if you took me seriously. But I do appreciate that you'd rather be fucked by me instead of four strange women. I might have felt emasculated otherwise."

She doubted Blaine Edwards could ever feel emasculated, but if he could, she'd want to be the one to do it to him. She eyed the large bulge at his crotch. All this talk about her with the other women had really turned him on. It kind of turned her on, too. She had been with women, but never more than one at a time. She still preferred men. Her mind latched onto something.

"So, you weren't serious about the whole sex slave thing either," she said.

"Nice try. That, I'm dead serious about."

He was being kind of placid about the whole thing. Was it just an act?

"You tricked me, so it doesn't count."

He gave her a sharp look. "I just passed up a *fivesome*. I'm not walking away empty-handed, babe."

She bit her bottom lip, wondering how much he regretted his loss. "Well, you got Charlene Johnson. That's more than a fair trade."

He slid onto the bed next to her and caressed the length of her arm. "Yes, it is."

She should've known he wasn't serious about the blackmail. Maybe she should say she wasn't serious about the sex slave thing, which she wasn't serious about. Was she? Damn. Being Blaine's sex slave. What would that entail? Had she really confessed her interest in BDSM? To Blaine Edwards of all people? No, it actually made sense. Like her, he was sexually adventurous. And he didn't seem to worry what anyone thought about it, either. She liked that. And she liked the light touch of his knuckles as he grazed the length of her bare arm.

"About the whole sex slave thing," she said. "I was under duress."

Damn, I feel like I went to college and shit.. She had never used the word "duress" before till she heard it on some cop and lawyer TV show. Audrey had explained what it meant.

"Fair enough," he said.

She started. He was going to let her off the hook just like that? She couldn't help but feel a little disappointed till he brushed his lips right below her ear. He nestled along her neck, to her shoulder, and softly kissed her beneath her jaw. The warmth in her belly began to percolate again.

"By the time I'm done, you'll be begging me to take you as my slave."

Her heart slammed into her chest. *Shit.* Did he mean that? Could he really make that happen? She got hotter and wetter thinking about it.

"You're a cocky son of a bitch," she said.

He kissed her throat. "I can see we're going to have a lot of fun with the whole BDSM thing."

"What the fuck are you talking about?"

He tongued the groove between her collar bones. "For one thing, you swear a lot."

"Like you don't?"

"Not as much as you."

"Well, you're special then, white boy."

He threaded his fingers into the hair near her temple and tugged her head back. "Yeah, that's got to go, too. Or you're going to get an ass-whupping so hard you won't be able to sit for days."

Her mouth fell open. *Shit.* The thought of getting spanked by Blaine was suddenly a big turn on. How the hell had that happened? Was it the rum and Coke? But, with his body hovering over hers, smelling the clean scent of his cologne or aftershave, and feeling his desire pulling at hers, she was pretty sure she couldn't blame it on the alcohol.

He released her and continued his gentle caressing of her throat, collarbone, and shoulders. He murmured into her neck, "I get the feeling you could be a real brat."

"What's that?"

"A brat. Someone who misbehaves on purpose to get punished."

Hmm. Could that be true? Would she want to get punished by him? She couldn't think straight right now. His kisses were distracting, but the pull in her womanhood wanted more than just kisses.

"Didn't I say something about wanting Blaine Edwards to fuck me?"

"You're not a patient girl. A little BDSM can take care of that, too."

"Don't call me 'girl.'"

"Woman," he corrected. "You are definitely all woman."

He cupped a breast through the thin material of her costume and passed his thumb over her nipple. The sensation shot straight to her pussy.

He looked her over from head to toe as he kneaded the breast. "'She makes hungry where most she satisfies.'"

"Huh?"

"It's from Shakespeare's *Antony and Cleopatra*."

"Hmmm. I bet Shakespeare was a lecherous old guy."

"He could be bawdy."

"I like bawdy. Probably should've paid more attention in English class."

He lightly pinched her nipple through the fabric. She arched her back and groaned. She loved nipple play. Intrigued by her response, he continued to fondle the nipple, sometimes gently, sometimes hard until she was writhing against the restraints. Her pussy ached.

"Oh, God," she breathed. "Suck it."

He pushed aside the fabric to reveal the glorious orb.

"Damn," he said.

"All natural," she said proudly. Her tits weren't overly large. They were a solid 36B and a perky pair.

He pulled the other breast from her top and devoured both spheres with his gaze. "They're perfect."

"What about me isn't?" she replied playfully.

"Speaking of cocky son-of-a-bitches..."

She raised a brow.

"But you got no complaints here," he retreated. "No complaints at all. Just awe. Total and complete awe."

He kissed around the areola of one breast and licked the nipple. "You taste good, too."

"Have more."

She arched her back, trying to shove more of her nipple into his mouth. She wished she didn't have the restraints on now so that she could grab his head and push him onto her nipple. He kneaded the other breast with his hand.

"Suck my nipple," she told him.

"I like a woman who's direct in bed."

"And I like men of action. You talk too damn much."

"What's the magic word?"

"You know you want to. Come on. Suck them."

"What's the magic word?" he repeated.

She huffed but relented. "Please."

He lapped at one nipple, then nipped it with his teeth. She gasped.

"Please suck my nipples."

Finally, he did what she asked and encased one in his mouth. He sucked. And suckled. Harder. Then softer. Then harder still. Each time he pulled the bud deeper into his mouth, the heat in her loins shot up a notch.

"Fuck! Yes!"

While he continued to suck on the one, he rolled and pinched the other nipple. She squirmed and gasped, and writhed and cried. She especially liked bumping into his hard body. As best as she could, she ground her pelvis at his crotch. His cock was definitely nice and hard. And she wanted it inside of her. Bad. Maybe she should never have let him tie her up. If she had her hands free and could press her body to his, he wouldn't be able to resist or take his sweet old time.

"Take your clothes off," she said. "Or, better yet, undo the cuffs and I'll take your clothes off."

"I don't know, Charlene. I kind of like you bound and completely at my mercy."

He gave her one of those smiles that probably would've melted most white chicks.

"Fine," she sighed. "But you are going to fuck me, right? I mean, you promised."

Once more, he reached a hand between her thighs and began to fondle her clit while he sucked her nipple. He soon had her twisting and bucking like crazy. Her body ached with wonderful, delightful, maddening desire.

"Jesus! Fuck me already!" she screamed.

"God, I love hearing you say that," he murmured into her breast.

Finally, he sat back on his haunches and pulled the white linen shirt over his head. Her gaze devoured his chiseled chest. Nice square pecs, a six-pack that narrowed to his hips. He was muscular, but not too beefy. Kind of reminded her of those naked Grecian or Roman statues. She couldn't wait to see the rest of him. He unbuttoned his pants with what seemed like deliberate slowness—or maybe it was just her impatience. She was salivating as he eased his pants past his hips.

Ooooh, baby. His cock came into view. Above average length, good girth. Nice flare to the head. Mostly straight, but ever so slightly curved. Course it mostly mattered how he used his tool and how long it would stay hard. But she wanted it inside of her. Now. Deep.

He rubbed his shaft. She expected him to smirk since he knew how much she wanted him now and was probably pretty proud of his shaft, but he seemed tentative. What the hell was the matter with him? Wasn't he as horny as she?

"I'm on the pill," she said in case that was what he was worried about, though she would have thought he, of all people, would've been prepared with a condom.

With an easy move, he was out of his pants and completely naked. If she had her hands free, she would have felt him all over. He covered her with his body and kissed her neck.

"Are you sure you want this?" he asked.

"What's the matter with you, boy? You want me to beg some more? That turn you on? Queen Cleopatra begging—"

He cut her off by smothering her mouth with his. His kiss was deep, and full, and probing. Caressing and demanding all at once. Like he was savoring and famished at the same time. She felt herself melt and spread her legs wider. He pushed aside the fabric between her legs and rubbed her there without relinquishing her lips. She liked the kiss—a lot—and thrust her tongue as deep into his mouth as she could. He didn't miss a beat and met her tongue like one of them male figure skaters catching his partner. But with his cock so close to her pussy—she could feel its hardness against her thigh—she could not focus on the kiss for long. She pushed her hips at him. He groaned. He shifted, and his cock was pointed at her slit.

Come on. Fuck me.

He pushed the head of his cock into her. She let out part of the breath she had been holding. She loved the feel of cock. So damn hard, yet in a way, so soft in its fit. Definitely better than a dildo. Slowly, he eased more of his cock into her. She flexed the walls of her vagina against his erection, feeling him, savoring him.

"Oh, God," he murmured, palming her breast.

Again she raised her hips, giving him the hint that she wanted more action. He returned to kissing her as he buried himself to the hilt.

Yes!

The kissing, the groping of her breast, the cock sliding in and out of her made her dizzy with arousal. The way he rolled his hips, the way he angled his penis inside her and drew it languidly against the bottom of her clit felt so damn good. So damn good. She barely had to do a thing. It didn't take her long to feel her climax coming, and maybe it was because she had already come once. Her pussy was clenching, and she started to buck her hips into him. They worked out a rhythm that had her arousal building fast and furious. The bed rocked beneath them as he thrust into her harder and faster until her grunts and pants turned into a cry. Her body trembled, her legs went into spasms, her arms strained against her bonds as all the pressure between her thighs was released in a delicious explosion.

When she finally surfaced from that lovely, easy orgasm, she realized he was still hard between her legs. She opened her eyes to meet his gaze. She had never noticed how pretty his blue eyes were, and how thick and full his lashes were.

He smiled at her. "We're not done yet, babe."

Audrey shivered, remembering how he had deprived her of sight at Trey's Naughty Noel with a similar red blindfold. She felt vulnerable not being able to see. At least this time he hadn't tied her hands together—yet. She forced herself to take a deep breath. He had brought a condom with him last time. She assumed he had one this time, too, but she made a mental note to double check when the time came. She could hardly believe she was doing this again, having sex with a complete stranger. At least he looked sexy in his Zorro outfit. She heard a rustling sound and wondered if he was removing his clothes and mask. Maybe the blindfold could slip and she'd get a glimpse of what he looked like. Or maybe it was better if she didn't see his face. He might be kind of ugly. At least right now, she could pretend he was gorgeous.

This time when he touched her, she felt his naked hand instead of a glove. He ran his thumb along her jawline. It moved to her mouth, tracing her bottom lip.

"Nice color," he whispered.

He had a faint accent—keeping up the Zorro impersonation, she supposed. Had he always had an accent and she simply hadn't noticed before?

"It's called Fuck-Me Red," she said. "Belonged to a friend of mine."

"Very appropriate."

His finger crooked beneath her chin and tilted her head up. Then his mouth brushed over hers. Her body tingled. How was it she could react so quickly to this stranger? He pressed his lips against hers more fully. The kiss was tender, as if he were savoring the taste and feel of her mouth. There was something familiar in the kiss, in the thorough way his mouth now worked hers, unrushed, varied, gradual, experienced. As if he knew her mouth, knew just when to tease her with a flick of the tongue, when to be gentle, and when to be assertive.

Despite having the blindfold on, she closed her eyes and gave herself into the kiss. He had graduated to a more possessive pressure, pushing his tongue into her mouth, disrupting her breath. Her body felt nice and warm, especially in the loins. He grasped her head on both sides. Over and over his mouth claimed hers, his tongue entwined hers, as he kissed her deep and full. Her body hummed. Damn. Zorro was a good kisser. When at last he eased the pace and withdrew, she wanted to cry, "More! More!"

He traced his knuckles down the side of her neck, along her collarbone, and down an arm. She shivered at his light touch, the promise of more to come. She knew of only one other man who could caress like that, who took his time and didn't try to grope her tits right away. Rance Durand. She felt his hand at her waist, pulling her closer to the edge of the bed. The hand slid down her thigh and the length of her boots.

"Nice boots."

"I got them special, just for you."

He grunted, and she couldn't decide if he approved or disapproved of her teasing. He put a hand to the back of her neck and kneaded away the tension. With both hands, he did the same with her shoulders and upper back.

"Mmmmm," she purred. "You're a masseur—or have been."

He made no response. Instead, he unzipped, very slowly, one of her boots. She felt his breath on her bare leg. He massaged her calf, reaching up her leg to just where the hem of her dress skimmed the middle of her thighs. He did the same with other boot and leg. The boots had covered so much territory, she felt as if she were practically naked without them. He put a hand to her shoulder and pushed her down onto the bed. His body was next to hers and he began kissing her once more. Wetness grew between her legs. Her back arched as he nestled and caressed her neck. Not being able to see, she didn't know where to put her hands. As if reading her mind, he took her hands and placed them over her breasts. She groped herself as he kissed her all about her neck, collarbone, and cleavage. His lips felt delicious on her. He wrapped an arm around her waist and pulled her body to him. She bent a leg atop his, and they locked lips vigorously, kissing long and deep till she was panting.

"*Mama mía*," she breathed.

The bed depressed and lifted as he got off. She heard something like a cork popping, then the sound of him rubbing his hands. She felt his hands, warm and slick with oil, on her arm. The oil had a sweet scent, like jasmine. It startled her at first, mostly because she hadn't been expecting that. It was a little disconcerting not to be able to see and anticipate. He waited for her surprise to pass, then massaged the oil into her arms and shoulders. Undoing the eye and hook closure at the back of her halter, he pulled the straps down, and rubbed the oil over her collarbone and the tops of her breasts. He did her legs and feet next, not missing an inch. When he was done, she felt completely relaxed. At the same time, her skin felt very alive.

He reached beneath her back and unzipped her dress. He tugged at the hem and dragged the dress down her body. She was naked before him, except for her red lace thong, a bright contrast to the rest of her outfit. She hadn't owned a lot of red lingerie, but Rance had liked the hue against her chocolate skin, so she had incorporated more of that color into her wardrobe. She wondered what Rance would have thought of her ensemble this evening. He would have liked it. All of a sudden, she wished he could have seen her looking all hot and erotic. He probably would have had her strut around naked with just the boots on. She remembered vividly when he had bought her her first naughty outfit from the little sex shop in the Castro.

"Oh!" she gasped in surprise when he palmed her breasts.

He kneaded the orbs, coating them well with the oil, rubbing, circling. When a hand brushed her nipple, she felt a zap of sensation between her legs. He lingered longer at her breasts, and the tension in her groin began to build. He applied the oil over her torso. She liked the feel of his strong hands on her waist and her belly, slowly going lower and lower, below her navel, entwining into the curls at the bottom of her pelvis. The massage had caused her blood to circulate throughout her whole body. When first he had removed her dress, she could sense the flames from the numerous candles, but the air in the room had not been particularly warm. Now she felt quite comfortable.

Reaching farther, his slick fingers found her mound. She groaned as he rubbed her there. *Oh yes, right there*. His fingers slid along her clitoris, the oil allowing him to glide swiftly against the sensitive bud. She moaned in delight. He pulled the thong aside and applied himself more energetically to her clit. Soon she was writhing and gasping. It felt every bit as wonderful as the first time he had masturbated her at Trey's Naughty Noel, every bit as wonderful as all the times that Rance had done it. At least physically. In her clit. There wasn't the happiness that filled her heart from experiencing pleasure from a loved one. There wasn't even a desire to reciprocate the pleasure, the way she had wanted to tear the clothes off Rance. With Zorro, she was mainly interested in what he was doing for her. This was purely carnal.

Her groaning became more urgent. He had found a particularly sensitive little spot in her clit and was now working it. She voiced her approval as he stroked her tirelessly. Her body hummed. The champagne and the massage had been good, preparing her for what was to come. And come she did. Her whole body jerked and trembled. He continued to caress her, milking her climax till it finally began to fade, his fingers staying with her. She sighed with contentment.

He flipped her onto her stomach. She felt his hands and the oil on her back and her neck. His touch was firm and eased the tension from her muscles. The massaging of her buttocks was particularly nice. To her surprise, he didn't seem in a hurry at all. Her mind drifted once more to Rance. He had given her a magnificent massage at his hotel, followed by some pretty amazing sex. She wondered why she was thinking of Rance so much. Was it because they'd had coffee together recently? Because she still didn't know what to do with the earrings he had gifted her?

Zorro turned her once more onto her back and ran his hands over every inch of her body in leisurely worship. It felt good to her, but she wondered if it was good for him. He seemed quite absorbed in what he was doing, and a few times she thought his breath sounded uneven. Eventually, he pulled his hands away. Instinctively, she put a hand to her blindfold to peek, but he stopped her hand. Holding her wrists together, he wrapped something soft, silk perhaps, around them, then pulled her arms overhead.

"Keep them there," he instructed.

She heard clothes rustling and assumed he was undressing. The bed sank with his weight. She felt him straddled around her waist. She wondered how naked he was. His legs were bare. She was curious to touch him but maybe it was better she didn't. What if he had a super hairy chest? That was one positive of black men—they tended to have nice, smooth chests.

He leaned over and kissed the side of her neck. Something stiff and hard, his cock, prodded her belly.

"You brought a condom?" she asked. "If not, I have one in—"

"Shhh. I have one. Do not worry."

He could have been lying, but there was such sincerity in his tone that she believed him. After kissing and tonguing the length of her neck, he turned his attention to her breasts, fondling their heavy fullness. He pressed them together. She felt his cock between them, gliding easily between the oiled orbs. She hoped he wouldn't come that way because she wanted to feel his cock inside of her. Though she had just come, she was already horny for her next orgasm.

He slid his hands from her breasts down her ribs and caressed her torso. She loved the feel of his hands. The skin was the body's largest organ, and he stimulated it oh so well. He lifted her left leg and ran his hands up and down the limb. He could do this all day, she thought happily to herself. He skimmed the side of her ass and groped a buttock.

"How 'bout you put that condom on now?" she asked.

"Sí, senorita."

She heard the tear of a condom wrapper, then felt his shaft between her legs. He stroked her clit with his cock, nice and slow at first, then with increasing vigor. Soon, she was panting and writhing, ready to come, but she wanted to come with some penetration. As if reading her mind, he sank his cock into her. Rance had always seemed to know exactly what she wanted, when she wanted it. She flexed her vaginal muscles around his member, making him groan. He began a gentle rocking thrust. She met his rhythm and they kept the missionary position for a while.

When she wanted him deeper, she angled her hips up and bent her knees. He raised himself higher and shoved his cock in to the hilt. His weight felt delicious on the back of her legs. He dragged his cock out, and the sensation on her g-spot made her teeth chatter. She wished she could grab onto the bed sheets or the headboard or him. When she tried to bring her arms down, he pulled them back above her. He grasped her left breast and tugged at the nipple.

"Oh God, oh Gawd, oh Gud," she mumbled incoherently as he shoved himself into her.

Knowing she was close to coming, she let him do all the work. Tension coiled tight in her loins. She let out a silent wail as her climax unfurled inside of her, spasming through her limbs, rattling her head, and accelerating her heart. Grunting, he pumped more furiously into her to achieve his own end. She felt him shudder. Her legs slid to the bed, and he lay on her for several minutes before planting a light kiss on her lips and withdrawing from her.

"Do not remove the blindfold," he told her.

She wondered what would happen if she did, but she remained where she was. She heard him getting dressed. He untied the restraint around her wrists.

"Don't move until I'm gone," he said.

The door opened and closed. She heard footsteps fading away. Removing her blindfold, she saw that she was alone. A shudder went through her. She couldn't believe she had had sex with a stranger again. But, damn, it had felt good. It was definitely more exciting than being at home with a vibrator. She passed a hand over her belly. Hopefully the oil would come off easily. She saw a folded towel on the corner of the bed. Had he left that for her? How very thoughtful. Like something Rance would have done.

She took the towel and began wiping the oil from her body. As she replayed her favorite parts of what had just transpired, she realized that Zorro had smelled awfully familiar.

12

What the fuck had she agreed to? Charlene stared at the ceiling of her apartment. Her stomach knotted at the thought, and her pussy clenched every time she replayed the different ways Blaine had made her come. Shit. She should not have gotten drunk at the party. But damn, the sex had been good. Almost as good as being with a brother. Unconsciously, she licked her lips.

Maybe Blaine had forgotten all about the sex slave thing. Maybe he was just messin' with her. Maybe he had been drunk, too, though he had seemed pretty sober. Or maybe he had moved on to more exciting things, like his gang bang with the four white chicks. After she and Blaine had emerged from their room, one of the girls had spotted him from the next room. Pretty soon all four of them were pulling him into the room, saying he owed them. Charlene wasn't sure how sincere his protests were.

"Have fun," she had said as she waved good-by as nonchalantly as she could, trying to quell a strange surge of jealousy.

She wondered what the four gal pals had done to Blaine. Nothing he wouldn't have wanted done. Images of them having group sex kept flashing through her mind. How many of them would he have been able to fuck at one time? Would they make him eat each of their pussies? Charlene touched herself, picturing Blaine eating her out. Something told her he might be pretty damn good at it. *Now, just because a guy has sex a lot, doesn't mean he's any good in bed*, she reminded herself. But Blaine had provided enough evidence to prove he wasn't all air when he bragged. He had been attentive, had fondled her in all the right ways, and made her come three times before he came.

Had she really asked him to fuck her? She rolled her eyes. Damn. She had probably come off desperate. And Charlene Johnson was not a desperate woman. It must have pleased his ego like nothing else to hear her say it. Damn alcohol. But she was a woman who spoke her mind. And she said what she wanted. Being tied to that bed, it had seemed the right thing to say. She liked being tied up, too.

She rubbed her clit faster.

But would she do it all over again? Hell, yeah. She'd go through all one hundred and one different sex positions with him.

No, not with Blaine Edwards. She had told him she wasn't going to screw around with him. Now she came off looking like one of those teases pretending to be hard to get. She couldn't stand those kinds of women.

Oh, well, that was the price she paid for being a sex fiend. It kind of made sense she'd fuck Blaine Edwards. He was the white, male version of her. She didn't have to worry about any hurt feelings or awkwardness with him. Except he was a friend of Rance. Maybe that would get awkward? Especially if something should work out between Audrey and Rance.

Nah, like her, Blaine could keep the sex and friendships separate.

Still, she felt a little funny about what had happened, though she had never regretted having sex before. But then, she had never agreed to be someone's sex slave before. What would he have made her do as his slave? Give him blow jobs whenever he wanted? Make her clean his house in the nude? Damn. The kinkiness of it was actually turning her on. She reached into her bedside dresser and pulled out her handy vibrator.

Ah, that was good. She focused on the humming of the vibrator against her. Then her mind went back to Blaine. She imagined herself riding him cowgirl style.

She'd have to tell him she was intoxicated and under duress—the more she used the word, the more she liked it. He couldn't hold her to it. The only thing he could do was void her certificate to Ballander's. She grimaced at the thought of it. Maybe she should just follow through with the sex slave thing after all. Pressing the vibrator harder against herself, she erupted into orgasm.

Audrey stared at the reflection of the purple balloon in the mirror. Oh wait, it wasn't a balloon. It was her dressed in lavender satin with an attached—what did that store woman call it?—crinoline.

"I like the spaghetti straps," Charlene offered from her chair as she sucked on a caramel lollipop, looking extra svelte next to the purple blimp.

"I could diet from now until the wedding and I'd still look fat," Audrey realized. She had an apple-shaped figure, and the poufy skirt only made it seem as if her fleshier top half continued to the bottom half.

The store assistant, a middle-aged blonde with her hair pulled tightly into a bun, popped her head into the dressing room. "How are we doing, ladies?"

"This dress definitely it?" Audrey asked, hoping against hope that it wasn't.

"It is. The bride and maid of honor were here yesterday to confirm the selection."

Audrey forced a smile. "Purple balloon it is."

Charlene peeked under the hem of the dress. "You could hide the flower girl and ring boy under that thing."

"I believe the bride is ready," the assistant announced.

Audrey and Charlene exited the dressing room and settled themselves before a circular area with a small podium surrounded by mirrors.

"Close your eyes," Izzy called from her dressing room.

Audrey did as told.

"Okay, you can open them now."

There was a collective gasp as they beheld Izzy in her gown of white with lace sleeves, a sweetheart neckline, and an open back that dipped to her waist. A lovely and slender Latina, Izzy would have looked beautiful in just about anything, but she looked exquisite in her wedding dress.

"Sooo...whadya think?" Izzy asked in a half-whisper.

Audrey blinked several times. "Wow. Just...wow."

"Sexy, sexy, sexy," Charlene said.

Izzy blushed. "I like it, too. Took me forever to find it. I mean, the wedding is in two months! You think Jan will like it?"

"Jan is gonna want to jump your bones then and there."

"It's definitely...wow," Audrey added. "You are going to be the prettiest bride in San Francisco."

Izzy let out a shaky breath. "Originally, I wasn't going to splurge on the dress. Jan didn't want to start our married life under a mountain of debt because we had a fancy wedding. But, I've saved up a little for something special, and isn't a wedding dress something special? I hope Jan won't be mad."

"Honey, every girl dreams of being a princess," the store assistant said. "Your wedding is your day to be princess."

Izzy bit her bottom lip.

"Jan's gonna be so bowled over, she's not gonna care how much you spent," Charlene said. "Tell her if she's gonna be upset, *I'll* marry you. Damn, I'd get married just to wear that dress."

"Yeah, right," Izzy returned, studying herself in the mirror.

Audrey could see the shine in her eyes and hoped along with her that Jan, the more frugal and practical of the couple, would take the price of the dress in stride.

"I'm serious. If I had me a man right now, I'd seriously consider it. Why not? You get tax breaks, right? And if you have the right partner, marriage doesn't have to change your lifestyle."

"I guess plenty of married couples swing and that kind of stuff."

The store assistant cleared her throat. "How do you plan to have your hair done?"

"Up but maybe in a low bun with a curl down the side."

"Sounds lovely. I have some veils that would go perfectly with that hairstyle."

"Or maybe I'd go for one of those red wedding dresses. Something different, you know," Charlene continued when the store assistant had left.

"You really would marry?" Izzy asked.

"Maybe. I'll have to see how you and Audrey do first."

"Me? That may be a while. If ever," Audrey said.

"I know you, girl. You may be Ms. Career and all, but you're a romantic underneath."

"I don't think so."

"That's 'cause you suppress it."

"Rance brought it out in you," Izzy said.

An awkward pause ensued.

Izzy flushed. "I'm sorry. I didn't mean—"

For some reason, Audrey felt a little perturbed but wasn't sure why. Forcing a small smile, she responded, "Don't worry about it. It's not like I can't talk about Rance or past relationships. Especially with my gals, right? He and I are grown-ups. *Mature* grown-ups. And we're not on bad terms or nothing."

"I don't get fancy earrings from my exes," Charlene said with mock ruefulness.

"He gave you earrings?" Izzy asked.

"For Christmas. He had bought them when we were in Hawaii," Audrey answered.

"Wow. He didn't have to do that."

"Yeah," Charlene piped with a sudden burst of energy, possibly from the sugar in her lollipop. "He coulda given 'em to that skinny white chick."

"I can see that might be kind of awkward if you bought a gift for one girlfriend and decided to give it to another."

"She wouldn't know. And that white girl is not really his girlfriend."

"What do you mean?" Audrey asked as if she were asking a purely intellectual question, like how did molecules separate and reform into new elements?

"They're not exclusive."

"How do you know?"

"Blaine said so. Besides, she don't look like Rance's type."

"She looks more his type than I do."

"Yeah, but Rance is different. He's European. Wouldn't be surprised if most men over there had some form of jungle fever. They probably don't come across many black women. We're, like, exotic and shit."

"Wasn't Josephine Baker European?" Izzy asked.

"Who now?"

Audrey stared at Charlene. "You don't know Josephine Baker? The famous French entertainer?"

"I don't do anything French 'cept French fries."

"Baker was actually African American. She moved to France and had a hugely successful career there."

"She refused to perform in front of segregated audiences," Izzy said, "and was active in the French Resistance during World War II."

"World War II!" Charlene exclaimed. "No wonder I never heard of her."

"Most people remember her for dancing practically naked with nothing but a skirt made of bananas," Audrey said. "But she was an outspoken civil rights advocate who spoke at the March on Washington with King. She was the NAACP Woman of the Year."

"And she was awarded the French Legion of Honor by Charles de Gaulle," Izzy added.

"Am I supposed to know this Charles dude, too?" Charlene asked. "And what's any of this got to do with Rance?"

"Why are we talking about Rance?" asked Audrey.

"If he was open to giving you guys another shot, would you do it?"

Audrey stared at her friend. Why was Charlene talking about this?

"He hasn't indicated he's interested."

"He gave you the earrings, remember? I'd say that's a pretty big sign. Gorgeous mother-fuckers, too. I swear if you don't wear them, I'll take them off your hands."

"It doesn't mean anything. What was he going to do with a pair of earrings?"

"He coulda given them to Stephanie. Or his mama. Doesn't he have a sister, too?"

"Maybe they don't like black pearls."

"Then he coulda donated them to a charity auction. Come on, girl. Ex-boyfriends just don't give their ex-girlfriends gifts outta the blue."

Audrey shifted uncomfortably, and not just because the crinoline was beginning to itch against her. "We're still friends."

"What kinda friend gives you mother-fuckin' gorgeous earrings for Christmas? *I* don't even give you shit like that."

"*You* don't give normal gifts at all. Hell, do you give anything that isn't shaped like a dildo?"

Charlene smiled broadly. "Gift cards for sex."

"I'd do earrings as a gift," Izzy said, "though I couldn't afford to give the kind Rance probably got you."

"See?" Audrey told Charlene. "It's perfectly normal."

Charlene turned to Izzy. "You'd get your ex fancy earrings for Christmas?"

Izzy faltered. "Well, no, especially now that I'm engaged. But a friend, sure."

"So you wouldn't give your ex no earrings because you'd be worried it'd send the wrong signal?"

"Right."

"But she'd give it to a friend," Audrey pointed out, now feeling a little irritated. "That's what Rance is—a friend."

Charlene sat back and crossed one slender leg over the other. "Un-hunh. You keep telling yourself that."

"What's your point?"

"I think Rance still has the hots for you. And you know you still got it for him because it was the best sex of your life. Said so yourself."

"Don't mean it can't happen with someone else. It already has."

Izzy perked up. "It has?"

Flushing, Audrey mumbled, "Oh, I didn't mention I went to some Eve of Erotica party with Charlene?"

"And made out with a stranger," Charlene elaborated. "Knocked boots in a serious way."

Izzy looked at Audrey. "You had sex with a stranger?"

A throat cleared and the three friends turned to look at the store assistant, who held two veils in her hands.

"This one has a layer that you can pull over your face," the woman said. "And this one actually pins at the base of the head."

Audrey glared at Charlene, hoping she was done talking about Rance now. But the woman had no shame.

"So which sex was better? Rance or the stranger?" Charlene asked as the store assistant pinned the first veil in place.

"We are *not* talking about this," Audrey said through gritted teeth.

"Why not? We all adults here."

"I am gonna smack you."

"What do you think?" Izzy asked with the veil in place.

Audrey and Charlene looked at the bride-to-be and melted at the same time.

"It's beautiful," Audrey answered. "It's perfect."

"I really do feel like a princess," Izzy said, her eyes watering. "I wish you could all get married, too!"

"Maybe if I could look half as good as you. You can see I don't do formal wear all too well."

Izzy looked sheepish. "Sorry about the bridesmaid dress. I could try talkin' to Rosa again."

"No, no. She's your maid of honor and your sister. If this is what she likes, I'm fine with it."

Izzy turned back to the mirror to admire herself. Audrey smiled for her friend. She couldn't be more happy for her friends Izzy and Jan. For a split second, she imagined what sort of wedding dress might make her feel as pretty as Izzy. And when she imagined walking down the aisle, it was Rance she pictured standing at the end.

"Stevenson & Young," Charlene said into the phone as she mindlessly twirled a pen between her fingers. "Ms. Jones is out of the office right now. Can I transfer you to her voicemail?"

After completing the call, she looked at the time display on the phone system. 2:47PM. She sighed. Five o'clock felt like a hundred hours away. She had hoped to ask Audrey to go to the gym with her after work so that they could continue their conversation about Rance. Audrey's great sex experience with the "stranger" at the Eve of Erotica had thrown a wrench in things. Why was it always so complicated with those two? Charlene also contemplated whether or not to tell Audrey about what had happened between her and Blaine. Audrey wouldn't approve, but she'd probably just confine herself to a roll of her eyes. She might eventually see the harmlessness and inevitability of two people dedicated to sex getting together. It didn't mean anything.

But the whole sex slave thing. Audrey might bug out on that one. Charlene had gone back and forth about it. At times, she thought, hell, why not go through with it? It sounded kinky, it was something she had never tried before. Blaine was good in bed. But for a whole week? And when he hadn't contacted her in over three days since the party, she had decided that if *he* had forgotten all about it, she wasn't going to remind him. Maybe he hadn't forgotten. Maybe he'd had second thoughts and didn't want to go through with it no more.

Charlene looked at the clock. 2:51PM. Maybe it was time for a quick break at the café downstairs. There was a mocha-caramel-choco-chip freeze with extra whip and her name on it. She reached into her desk for her purse and put the "Back in 15 minutes" sign on the counter. The phone rang.

"Stevenson & Young."

"Don't do it."

A shiver went up her spine. It was Blaine. "Don't do what?"

"That drink with five thousand calories."

What was he, some kind of fuckin' mind reader?

"I know you're thinking of getting one," he went on to say.

A little irritated that he was right and that he had taken so long to call her, she lowered her voice and said with some exasperation: "What you want, white boy?"

"Okay, we gotta get some ground rules straight. It's not 'white boy,' it's 'Sir.'"

Her heart rate quickened and she glanced around to see if anyone was within earshot. "Whachyou talkin' about?"

Damn, she did not just come off sounding like Gary Coleman from *Different Strokes*.

There was a pause before he answered, "You already know I'm not the PC sort of guy. I leave that to Alan and Rance. But I will change the term 'sex slave' to 'submissive' 'cause I get that 'slave' is a loaded word."

She found it difficult to swallow. So he hadn't forgotten. But then why take more than three days to contact her? Was he playing one of those games where he pretended not to be too interested in her by not calling too early? She shouldn't even care. She better not show that she cared or even noticed.

"You're not serious," she tried. "I mean, that was fun dirty talk an' all, but—"

"I don't fool around like that. I'm dead serious about you submitting to me for a whole week. Been thinking about it all weekend."

"Yeah? Then why'd you wait until today to call me? It's Tuesday."

She could hear the smile in his voice. "Missed me?"

Shit. She had just done what she didn't want to do: revealed that she had noticed.

"You wish," she retorted, and just to get under his skin, added, "white boy. I was expectin' you to tell me that you were just joking."

"I had to fly down to LA unexpectedly. A company we gave some venture funding to appears to have cooked its books."

"You could've texted."

"Suspense and delayed gratification can intensify sexual pleasure."

She felt a throb between her legs. What should she do? Should she argue her way out of it?

"I was pretty drunk."

"But you're not now."

"So?"

"If you want out, fine. I respect people don't make the best decisions when they're drunk. But if you're in, we can start the week right now. I'm not gonna push it because I promised I'd stop hitting on you if you got Audrey to the Eve of Erotica. But you're as sexually adventurous as I am, and I know you enjoyed what I did that night, so this could be a pretty fun week for you."

She took a fortifying breath, wishing she had come up with a game plan before he called. She didn't like being at a loss. It wasn't typical for her. She waited for some light bulb to go off. Submit to Blaine Edwards for a whole week? Call him 'Sir'? Could she really do it? She had toyed with a little S&M before, but she had played the part of a dominatrix.

Despite the long silence, Blaine didn't say anything. Not even a "Well?" to prompt her.

"You still there?" she finally said.

"Take your time."

"Fine."

"'Fine,' you'll do it?"

"But I want out at any time. I'm not gonna do it for a whole damn week if it gets boring and shit."

"I promise it'll be anything but boring."

She let out a breath. Her body was on edge.

"What are you doing after work?" he asked casually.

"Hittin' the gym to burn off the calories from my mocha-caramel-choco-chip freeze. See, I pay attention to what I eat."

"Those are empty calories. You fill yourself on that, you won't have an appetite for calories with nutrition. What are you doing after the gym?"

"Grab dinner on the way home. There's a food truck around the corner with the best chimichangas—"

"You always eat like this?"

"Look, rich boy, I don't have a chef working for me or anything like that."

"I don't either—always. This is what you're going to do: you're going to skip the mocha-caramel-choco-chip freeze, but you'll go to the gym for an hour. I'll pick you up from there."

"You takin' me out to dinner?"

A list of the city's finest restaurants started scrolling through her mind.

"No. We're going back to your place."

"Oh," she said, highly disappointed.

"But if you do well, I'll take you to *Benu.*"

She cheered up.

"But if you misbehave and call me 'white boy' or 'rich boy' or any-other-kind of 'boy,' I've got a flogger with your name on it."

Another shiver went through her.

"Got it?"

So here we go. Part of her resisted the obvious answer. Submitting to Blaine was not going to be easy.

"Got it?"

"Yeah, yeah."

"'Yeah, yeah, 'Sir.' Remember?"

To her surprise, heat now swirled in her lower abdomen. He had dropped the term "slave," but she wasn't sure 'Sir' was any better. She took a deep breath.

"Yes, Sir."

13

Blaine hung up his cell, let out a breath, and killed the water in his glass. During the long silence as he'd waited for Charlene to answer, he'd taken half a dozen sips of water to prevent himself from speaking and appearing too eager. As the weight of what had transpired sunk in, he couldn't help a triumphant smile. Charlene Johnson was going to submit herself to him for a week! Provided he made it worth her while. And he was going to make it worth her while. No question. He felt stoked, as if the 49ers had won the Super bowl.

"The delay of materials from China is going to set us back a month on the dining room," Rance said when Blaine reentered the meeting room at the *Hotel sur Mer*.

"That sucks," Blaine replied. "Aren't we already bumping up against tourist season?"

"We should still make it. I always factor delays into the timeline."

"'Course."

Sitting at the table, Blaine scrolled through his email on his Blackberry to see if there was word from the auditor going through the books of one of his investments.

"Are you nervous about something?" Rance asked, staring at Blaine's knee.

Looking down, Blaine realized his knee was rapidly agitating up and down. He willed it stop. "Excited, I guess. I got myself a week with Charlene."

"Congratulations. I didn't think she would give in."

Blaine grinned broadly. "All women do eventually. I'm pretty irresistible."

"What was the bribe?"

"Ouch, dude."

Blaine was feeling pretty good about himself. Putting down his Blackberry, he leaned back in the chair with his hands behind his head.

"Nada."

"Nothing?"

"Nothing. I didn't bribe her with anything. Had to coax her into getting Audrey to the Eve of Erotica with a year of dining at Ballander's, and I promised not to hit on her anymore, but the week of submission didn't cost me a dime."

Rance stared at his friend with skepticism.

"Thanks for the vote of confidence," Blaine said.

Rance folded his arms and leaned against the wall. "I just thought Charlene had higher standards."

"Keep it up and I won't finance your fancy-ass kitchen. Seriously, it makes sense. She's into sex. I'm into sex. She's hot. I'm hot."

"What is a week of submission?"

Blaine leaned forward and rested his forearms on the table. "She agreed to be my sex slave."

"What?"

"Well, submissive. Sort of the same."

"Get out of here."

"I'm serious, dude. Can't quite believe it myself, actually."

"Wow. I can't believe she agreed—with *you*."

"You're beginning to sound like Alan."

"Your sex slave. That's kinky stuff."

"I know. It starts today. I'm gonna pick her up from the gym."

"Then what?"

"I don't know. I thought she was gonna beg out of it 'cause she was drunk at the Eve of Erotica. Speaking of which, how did it go with you?"

"Fine."

"Meaning you rocked her world."

"As far as she knows, some stranger dressed as Zorro rocked her world."

"So? Let her know it's you."

Rance ran a hand through his hair. "I can't. She might not be happy to know it's me."

"So find out."

"My family has been asked to come in on an acquisition in Hong Kong. It would be good if I could fly out there in three weeks."

"How long you gonna be there?"

"At least a couple of weeks. Maybe longer."

"What about the *sur Mer*?"

"That's where you come in, my friend."

"Shit. You're lucky you let me cheat off your stats homework while we were at Stanford."

"I did what?"

Blaine leaned back in his chair again. "Guess you never noticed."

Rance shook his head. "You're twice as good with numbers as I am. You didn't need to cheat off my homework."

"Yeah, but you always had yours done first, so it was just more efficient that way. I had places to go and people to see."

"You mean Trisha's room, and Kelly's room, and Veronica's room..."

"Like I said, places to go and people to see. Did you know Trisha's back in San Francisco? Divorced now. Our sophomore year, she and I were in the steam tunnels once, thought about breaking into the President's office, but decided to make out instead. I think she had it pretty bad for you, too."

"We need to go over some more details of the remodel before I leave for Hong Kong."

"If you're gonna be gone that long, you should talk to Audrey."

"Why? I don't think she's interested in getting back together."

"Sure she is."

"And how would you know this?"

Blaine shrugged. "When have you not had a woman want to be with you? 'Cept that Chinese chick whose dad didn't approve of you 'cause you weren't a billionaire at the time. Who'd she end up marrying?"

"Tony Zhang."

"Oh right. His net worth is $3.8 billion. DHRG is only $1.6 billion."

Rance flipped through some documents at the table. "I might meet with the guy when I'm in Hong Kong. His family is redeveloping the properties across from the hotel."

"Is your ex gonna be there?"

"I don't know. It doesn't really matter. Hannah and I dated very briefly."

"Her family's worth a couple billion, too, right?" Blaine could see his question didn't interest Rance. He decided to go back to a previous topic. "So you gonna tell Audrey or not?"

"I thought we went over this already."

"Maybe I'll get Charlene working on it. She's got to do what I tell her."

Rance shook his head. Blaine glanced at the clock. He could hardly wait to get her text letting him know she had finished working out at the gym. After her workout, she was going to hit the shower. He could feel his cock stiffen just picturing Charlene in the shower, the water flowing over her hot body, the suds decorating her full breasts, sliding down her smooth abs, and over that luscious fuckin' ass. He had given her his first directive as "Master." To ready herself, she was to masturbate while taking the shower.

"Until you come," he had said.

"Seriously?" she had returned. "That could take a while. I don't want my skin to get all prunie."

"Just be glad I'm not telling you to play with yourself right now beneath your desk."

There had been a long pause.

"Fine. I'll do it. But only for so long. Like I said, I don't want my skin to get all prunie."

"I'm gonna like the part where I get to spank you good for not following orders."

Yes, sirree. He would like the spanking a lot. Her ass was made for spanking. His cock reared its head at the prospect.

"I need some water with ice," he told Rance. "Lots of ice."

The steam of the shower curled all around her. Charlene worked the bath gel into a lather and smoothed it over her arms. Blaine had told her to play with herself in the shower. Part of her didn't want to do it. She still wasn't sold on the idea of taking orders from him. She brushed the lather over her boobs. It wasn't like he would know whether she did or didn't. She could just lie and said she did. But what if he figured she was lying? What would he do? She looked down and admired her peaked nipples. Once more, she passed a hand over a breast. She tugged a little at her nipple. What would Blaine do with her tonight? She cupped a breast. Would they fuck? Of course they would. A warmth separate from the hot water collected beneath her navel.

She was going to be his submissive for a week. Maybe she should have asked him what exactly that entailed for him. Was he into S&M shit, too? She considered herself pretty sexually adventurous, but she hadn't tried any intense stuff. Shit. Now she felt kinda stupid for not asking what she was getting into. Wasn't there supposed to be rules? Limits? Yeah, she was pretty certain that was the protocol. They'd have to have a sit down before starting anything. They'd have to agree to terms or she was out.

For now, as she fondled one breast, she might entertain the idea of masturbating because he had told her to. She slid her hand between her thighs. Mmmm. Her body was ready. Maybe she could get him to just fuck her without all the submission stuff. She was pretty sure she could seduce him into that. She kinda liked the idea of that challenge. Blaine wouldn't be able to resist her. He'd see who was really in command.

She stroked herself a little harder. Maybe she'd tie him to the bed this time. She licked her lips at the thought of his delicious body spread-eagle, a limb pulled to each bedpost. She'd tease him good, starting with the nipples. She'd caress and grab all those taut muscles. Then she'd focus in on his cock. Maybe blow it some.

She surprised herself with a moan. She wanted to come. Her body was definitely aroused now. Leaning against the shower wall, she spread her legs and rubbed herself faster. She pictured herself straddling him. She bet she could ride him better than anyone. How good it would feel to grind her clit into his pelvis! She bucked her hips into her hand. If only he were here now. If only it was his dick and not her hand between her legs. While one hand slid along her clit and pussy, the other played with her breast again. She could feel the tension in her body peaking. Her legs tensed. She almost cried out as the tremors of her climax went through her. She sagged against the wall and leaned her head back. That was good, but she couldn't wait for the real thing.

"Hey, you almost done in there?" a voice asked from the other side of the shower door. "There's only two working showers, you know."

"Chill. I'll be done soon," Charlene replied, peeling herself from the wall.

She finished her shower and after putting some product in her hair and blow-drying it, she pulled on her skinny jeans, a burgundy sweater with a low neckline, and a pair of tall leather boots. She turned every single head as she walked out of the gym. Outside, she spotted Blaine leaning against his car, working on his Blackberry. In a button-down shirt, khakis, and a jacket, he was a little more dressed up than she was used to seeing. The breeze caught his blonde hair and whipped it over his brow. She wondered what it would be like to have thin, fine hair. When he looked up and smiled with boyish enthusiasm, she could see how white women fell for him all the time.

"That was a long shower," he commented as he took her gym bag and popped the trunk. "Cost me twelve bucks."

"Well who told you to park right up front—and during prime time," she shot back, though she was known to park illegally just to get as close to her destination as possible. She allowed him to open the car door for her. It was the one thing she insisted on from a guy. If he didn't open the door for her, he wasn't ever gonna make it past first base.

"So, did you do what I asked?" he asked after they were seated in the car.

She looked around the car. It was a simple Audi coupe. Not what she would have expected from a guy with his kind of money. But it was a hybrid.

"Yeah, I did," she answered as if it was no big thing and she did it all the time.

He glanced at her from the sides of his eyes before shifting the car into drive. "Good. The master-submissive relationship is pretty simple. Do what I tell you, get rewarded. Misbehave, get punished."

She eyed him. "You've done this kind of thing before? I mean, just cause you went to the Citadel Club a few times..."

"I dated a Domme for a while. She taught me a lot. I'm still surprised you haven't been to the Citadel."

She pursed her lips. Did that mean she wasn't as sexually adventurous as he was?

"I been to a swingers' club."

"Yeah? Did you like it?"

"It was cool. I had one boyfriend who was into that kind of stuff."

"What'd you do there?"

"Did a ménage-a-trois a couple of times."

"With two guys?"

"My boyfriend and one of his exes. He liked to watch us make out."

"Shit."

"What's the matter?"

"Missed the turn." He pulled the car into the driveway of a warehouse and backed out. "You can't tell me shit like that when I'm driving, babe."

She suppressed a smile, enjoying how she could discombobulate him. "You asked."

"I did. So you might as well tell me the whole thing. How'd you two make out?"

"We'd both be naked. I like to be on top."

"You like making out with another woman?"

"Sometimes. I like it when our boobs touch and our nipples tickle each other."

She could see his grip on the steering wheel tighten. Emboldened, she continued, "I kinda like kissing a woman. Soft lips, no rough edges. I can usually get my tongue nice and deep into a woman's mouth."

Blaine groaned. "You ever go down on a woman?"

"Sure. But I don't want to get us into an accident."

He took a haggard breath. "Yeah. Let's change the topic."

"Nice weather we're having," she responded, affecting a stiff white tone.

The fog had rolled in, and the air had started to mist. He shook his head but smiled.

"Let's go over the rules then. I like to keep things simple. One: you call me 'Sir' at all times. Two, you thank me for everything I do. Three, you ask permission for anything and everything."

"What? Like I gotta ask you if I need to go piss?"

"You got it. At least when I'm around. We don't do anything you don't want, so if you have any limits, just say so. Some people don't like caning or fisting or piercing. We'll also use a safety word. What do you want it to be?"

Her mind reeled at the images. She already knew she wasn't a pain freak.

"Fuck," she exhaled.

"That won't work. We'll be doing too much of that for me to tell if you're using it in the context of the safety word. Pick something that can't be confused."

Her mind drew a blank. The only word that popped into her head was "cotton candy."

"Cotton candy it is," he said.

With his right hand on the wheel and left arm propped casually on the door, he looked so much more relaxed than she felt. The *idea* of BDSM was erotic, naughty, exciting. But would it prove that way in reality? She let out a small, shaky breath.

"Hey," he said softly, reaching for her knee and giving it a gentle squeeze, "this is supposed to be fun, not scary. Maybe a little scary, but in a sexy way."

"I know," she snapped. "You don't scare me, white boy."

"Ooooh. That's gonna cost you, babe."

"Cost me what?"

"You'll see."

She shifted in the leather seat and said nothing as he pulled the car up to her apartment complex.

"How'd you know where I live?" she asked as he waited for her to find the garage door opener. "You stalk me or something?"

"It was easy. A friend of mine has the voter rolls. It's public information. You need to vote more, by the way. You haven't voted since the last presidential election."

She crossed her arms. "You givin' me a civics lesson?"

"Don't you care what happens in this city? This state?"

"'Course I do."

"Then vote."

"Why? Democrats always win around here."

"There are different shades of Democrats—especially in San Francisco. If you're the wrong kind of Democrat, you might as well be a Tea Party member to some. And there's more on the ballot besides candidates."

She narrowed her eyes at him. "This isn't gonna last long if I have to sit through lectures. Just 'cause you went to Stanford an' shit don't mean you know best about everything."

"If I didn't think you were smart, I wouldn't be telling you to vote. Voting is a right for every citizen, but that doesn't mean every citizen ought to exercise it. Dumb people should stay home on election day. Now open up the gate."

She jabbed her clicker, and the iron gate began to roll open. "I can quit if you get too annoying."

"Sure," he smiled. "Lucky for you I have other talents. You'll want to stick it out, annoying civics lessons and all."

His smile was infectious, but she suppressed her smile, grumbling, "Maybe, maybe not."

Once parked, he grabbed a duffle bag from his trunk and they took the elevator to the tenth floor. He stood close by her as she unlocked the door of her unit. She was glad to be inside because his nearness rattled her. It didn't rattle her before.

She dropped her purse on the floor and tossed her keys on the kitchen counter.

"Whoa," he said as he stepped over the threshold and saw the clothes and magazines strewn all over the living room. "My dorm room didn't look as messy. And I shared one with two other guys."

"I have a small place."

"Where do you want me to set this?" he asked, holding her gym bag.

"By the door is fine."

He pushed aside a laundry basket to make room for the bag. "How do you find anything around here?"

"Look, we gonna fuck first or eat first?"

He grinned. "I like how you cut to the chase. You hungry?"

"Yeah."

Working out always gave her an appetite and she would have stopped by the smoothie place next to the gym for a chocolate-peanut-butter shake if Blaine hadn't been waiting for her.

"Let's see what you got." He opened up the refrigerator.

She couldn't help feeling a little disappointed that they weren't going out. With a sigh, she sat herself down on the barstool on the other side of the kitchen counter.

"A leftover grilled cheese sandwich, chocolate milk, and condiments," he listed. "Haven't you heard of fruits and vegetables?"

She shrugged. "I'm not much of a cook."

He opened the freezer. "TV dinners, a frozen pizza, ice cream, a frozen cheesecake, and—tater tots? What is this? Food for eight year olds?"

"You gonna make fun of my food all night?"

"No wonder you like eating out."

Ignoring him, she pulled out a take-out menu. "There's a Chinese place downstairs. They make a great Mongolian beef."

He closed the refrigerator and unzipped his duffle bag. He pulled out red and yellow bell peppers and fresh basil.

"Wasn't sure what you had, and I passed by the Crocker Galleria farmer's market," he explained.

She eyed the vibrant colors of the vegetables. Was he expecting her to cook?

"I thought your bag had sex toys or BDSM shit," she said.

"From what I understand, you got plenty of sex toys." He pulled out a box of penne, olive oil, and grated cheese.

"But not BDSM shit. Except for handcuffs. And a spreader bar."

"We can improvise."

His response perked her curiosity, but she decided to save her questions for later. For the moment, she wanted food. She watched him pull out a pot and fill it with water. "You cook?"

"A few simple dishes. Just enough to impress the chicks."

"I dated a chef once. Real hot mother-fucker. I used to think chefs were fat, short European dudes. But we didn't last long."

"Let me guess. He couldn't stand your eating habits."

"Smart ass. *I* dumped *him*. The guy was a vegan. What kind of mother-fuckin' chef is a vegan? And in San Francisco, where you can find some of the best fuckin' food anywhere. I couldn't eat anything in front of the guy without feeling guilty."

"You weren't ready to give up your burgers for him?"

"No man is worth giving up meat. Not red meat anyway. I take that back. Southern fried chicken—real good Southern fried chicken—where the skin is crispy and the meat is all moist and juicy inside—that's as good as a filet mignon any day. What? What are you staring at me for? Maybe you never had yourself good fried chicken."

He had a glazed look in his eyes. "No, it's just the way you talk about food. Fuckin' hot. We might have to fuck first."

"Bring it on, white boy."

Gleefully, she watched him drop the knife and bell pepper and round the corner to where she sat. His hand went around her neck and his mouth came crashing down on hers. She returned the kiss with aggression, wanting to make sure he knew she wasn't no wimpy kisser. Arousal had flared surprisingly fast. Maybe it was cause she had jacked off in the shower at the gym and come only once. Once wasn't usually enough for her.

He kept pace with her kissing without getting too slobbery. She had to give him props for his skill there. In fact, he soon tamed her onslaught. She was pressing her lips hard to his, delving her tongue deep into his mouth. But with his hand at the base of her head, he took the helm and navigated her mouth and tongue at his leisure. Her insides melted, and she grudgingly relinquished control to him. She grabbed his head and wound a hand through his hair, and felt a stab of regret that he would not get to feel the same softness with hers. She pulled him into her, wanting his tongue to probe and touch the desire building within her.

His other hand wrapped itself around her back, caressing. She shivered in delight. She loved it when a guy worshipped every part of her body. His hand felt good on her. His kisses grew in urgency, and so did the heat between her legs. She scooted her hips closer to him and started unbuttoning his shirt. She wasn't sure why she was so turned on right now. Maybe it was because she was hungry. She should be irritated with him more than anything. The guy had lectured her and made fun of her eating and living habits. The cocky son of a bitch. But here she was, wanting a piece of him.

He undid the buttons of his cuffs, and she slid the shirt off. She saw a glimpse of him in his undershirt before he claimed her mouth again. Wrapping her legs around him, she could feel his erection nice and hard against her inner thigh. She moved her legs to rub against it. He groaned and deepened the kiss. Her panties were already slightly damp from her earlier masturbation, now they were soaked. Without relinquishing her lips, he held her by the legs and carried her into the bedroom, nearly stumbling over a pair of shoes before falling into the bed with her. She had a nice queen-sized sleigh bed. She usually didn't make her bed in the mornings, and the cover and sheets were in disarray. She had different piles of clothes all over the place, some were garments she had tried on earlier in the day but decided not to wear, others were clothes she had worn briefly but not long enough to warrant going in the laundry. For a second, she regretted not having tidied up a bit, but she reminded herself that she was not out to impress Blaine.

As his hands roamed and caressed her body, it was clear her mess didn't have any dampening effect on him. She arched her neck so that his mouth had full access. He kissed his way down her throat to her cleavage. He pushed a breast up and caressed the exposed top of the orb.

"Mmmm," he moaned as he grabbed her ass with his other hand.

She wrapped one leg behind him, enjoying the weight of his body on hers. He went back to kissing her mouth while he groped her. Used to having men attack her titties first, she wanted him there and arched her back, pushing her breasts into him. But he took his sweet time. He caressed her back, her ribs, her bent legs till she was writhing in need for more. At last, he slipped a hand beneath her top and cupped a breast through her lacey bra. He found the nipple and rolled it between his thumb and forefinger. The lace tickled her, and an electric shock zipped from the sensitive bud straight into her pussy. He lifted the hem of her top over her bra and paused to admire the view.

"I'm usually a legs and ass guy, but these are gorgeous."

She couldn't help a grin. She may not be the smartest, definitely wasn't wealthy or nothing, but she had her assets, ones she wouldn't trade for anything at the moment.

Slipping a finger into the lace cup, he pulled it down to bare the breast. He cupped it and squeezed the pliant flesh. Lowering his head, he engulfed her nipple. The warmth and heat of his mouth made her moan. He licked at the bud gently and tenderly, sucking it occasionally.

"Harder, baby," she urged.

She gasped when he obliged. He sucked in earnest, lapping at the areola, digging his fingers into the flesh. She ground her hips at him in approval. The attention on the one nub was making another, lower down, pulse with need. It was getting too much for her. She needed more. Sensing her impatience, he sat back and pulled off her boots. She rubbed her own crotch. God, she was feeling horny. Probably that time of the month when her menstrual cycle was peak baby-making time. He watched as she tried to create some pressure against her clit.

"You are so fucking sexy," he said, his voice low and guttural.

Encouraged by the lust shining in his eyes, she unbuttoned her jeans and slipped her hand inside. He pulled her hand back out.

"No, no. That pussy is mine. You don't get to touch it unless I give you permission."

She pouted, having forgotten they were doing the whole dom and sub thing.

"But you can take your jeans off," he said.

She wiggled out of the pants with his help. The jeans were probably a size too small, but she had liked how they looked on her. He caressed the length of her leg.

"Wow," he whistled. "You shave well."

"Haven't you been with a black woman before? We don't get hairy legs."

"I've been with black women, but they didn't have legs this smooth unless they shaved."

She didn't know why, but she felt a little jealous. It might have been kind of cool to be the first black woman Blaine had ever been with.

"Maybe they weren't black enough," she shrugged. She probably shouldn't ask, but she was too curious. "How many black women you been with?"

He lifted her leg and began kissing her calf. "Two, maybe three. The last one was kind of hard to tell. She was part Filipina, too, I think."

"And the other two?"

"Jade. At Stanford. She plays for the WNBA now. And Tammy."

"Shit. She can't be black. No black woman named Tammy."

"This one was."

"Must've been adopted."

He crawled back on top of her and kissed the soft spot beneath her jaw. She shivered.

"Surprised you remember their names," she murmured.

"I'm good with names," he said as his lips passed over hers.

She suddenly realized he had unclicked her bra, and she hadn't even noticed. *Figures, he's probably done that more times than he can count.*

His hands continued to grip and fondle her, activating every nerve in her body. She had heard or read somewhere that the brain was the most important sex organ, but her skin, which was the single largest organ of the body, made for great foreplay, especially the way Blaine handled her. When he pulled her top and bra off, she was ready to jump him if he didn't take her soon. She reached for his undershirt, wanting him to be as naked as she was. He helped her take it off, and she licked her lips at his sculpted chest. She liked hairless chests, so she was glad to see he had smooth pectorals. She liked to see and play with man nipples. He had a nice six pack without being too lean or beefy. Some men had such hard ridges in their abdominal muscles, they reminded her of an ice tray. Blaine actually could've been a model.

"May I kiss your nipples, Sir?" she asked with exaggerated demureness.

He smiled. "You may."

Leaning in, she licked at one. *Yummy.* She licked again, then sucked it till it was nice and hard. Her appetite flared and she went at the bud nice and good.

"Enthusiastic, aren't you?" he said after a little groan.

She caressed his pectorals and his sides just as he had caressed her. For a white guy, he was pretty tasty. The more she sampled, the more she liked. Her hands fell to his belt. He watched as she undid the belt, the button of his pants, and his fly. She stroked the bulge she had revealed. She liked his underwear: something like boxers but form fitting, like tighty-whities. She pulled his pants down past his hips. While he shed everything except his underwear, she massaged her own breasts.

"I like that you like touching yourself," he remarked.

She grinned. "I like touching myself, too. Can't help it I'm so hot I turn myself on."

It was the truth. She liked her own body. Probably one of the few women in America who did. That's why she considered herself damn lucky.

"I gotta see that fine ass of yours now."

Giddy, she promptly got on all fours with her backside to him. She was wearing lacey boy shorts, and they revealed just the right amount of flesh to entice. She wiggled her butt for effect. He whistled.

"So, whadya think? Hottest piece of ass in the City?"

"You're selling yourself short, babe. It could be the hottest ass in the world."

She couldn't help but smile. She liked the compliment. He grasped one cheek—hard.

"Betcha want a piece of it," she teased.

"Yeah."

His voice sounded a little hoarse.

"Take 'em off," he ordered.

Hooking her thumbs into the underwear, she gradually shimmied them down her butt. She turned her head to see his expression. He looked like a wolf who hadn't eaten in days. She let the panties rest at the bottom of her rump. He palmed a buttock and brushed his thumb over the curve. He pulled the panties down.

"Soaking wet," he observed. "Like 'em that way."

The panties pooled around her knees. He slid his hand between her legs and stroked her folds. She was very wet.

"I like an ass fuckin' but not on the first time," she informed him.

"It's not our first time."

"I mean, you gotta work up to it. I don't mind being slutty, but I don't give up my booty to just anyone."

"You're killing me, babe."

"A girl's got to have standards. I ain't no street hoe."

He palmed her rear, ran his hand up her back and into her hair. He yanked it, gently, and whispered in her ear. "What if I just take it?"

Her heart leaped into her throat. He was just playing a role, but, *damn boy*, it had sounded real.

"After all, it's mine for a week," he added.

Her pussy throbbed. She couldn't think of a response.

"But first, you're due some punishment, babe."

14

Blaine didn't see but he sensed her eyes widen. She had either forgotten or maybe she had thought he was going to let things slide. He was a little ticked that she had forgotten that their first time had been at the New Year's Eve of Erotica party. Or maybe she hadn't forgotten, just made it sound as if she had forgotten. Either way, it was messed up. Well, he was going to make sure she didn't forget tonight.

Damn, the woman was luscious. Seeing her on all fours on the bed, completely naked, it was a miracle he didn't throw himself at her. He rubbed her incredible ass.

"Hold still," he instructed.

"Hold still for what, white boy?" she asked, her voice tinged with a little trepidation.

"I told you not to call me 'white boy.'"

She shrugged. "Old habits are hard to break."

He smacked her hard on one buttock. She gave a loud gasp. Her butt muscles were taught but the flesh quivered for a second. Seeing it made his cock throb.

"Fuck!" she swore. "You could have told me you were going to spank me that hard."

"I'm just warming up, babe."

Her large brown eyes grew even bigger.

"I know you been spanked before. C'mon, take it like a good girl. Maybe next time you'll remember not to call me 'white boy.'"

He slapped her equally hard on the other buttock.

"Fuck!" she yelped. "You like 'asshole' better?"

"Christ, you're difficult."

He spanked her even harder. She made a move as if she was about to turn away and sit down to protect her ass from him, but he put a quick hand to the back of her head and pressed her down into the pillows, not harshly, but enough for her to know who was in charge. He had to be careful not to frighten her too much, but he figured Charlene could take it.

"Now I know you're ready for a fucking," he said, caressing her again between the thighs while he continued to hold her down, "so I wouldn't delay too much."

She groaned when his fingers found her clitoris. "You want it just as much as I do, wh—"

She caught herself.

"See? You can learn new habits."

Still holding her head down, he smacked her rump with the full force of his left hand. Lucky for her, he was right-handed. But it still smarted.

"In fact, I think you owe me an apology for those racial slurs."

"Fuck you."

Oh boy. She wanted to do it the hard way. Well, she had asked for it. He had to show her who was the Dom, and in a way that made it clear who held the reigns. He had already cut her a lot of slack. No self-respecting Dom would have let her get away with it all, so he had ground to make up. Going from nice guy to hardass didn't work, but going from hardass to nice guy generated gratitude. One had to set the tone from the beginning.

Taking a deep breath and calling on the Method techniques he had learned in drama class, he yanked her up by the hair.

"What did you say?" he asked in her ear.

"You know I didn't mean it as a racial slur. 'Fact, it could be like a—whadya call it—term of endearment. Like black men calling each other 'nigga.'"

"Bullshit. You don't mean it like that at all."

The look on her face confirmed his belief. He grabbed her bra. It didn't have any underwire, so it worked well for his purpose. He used it to bind her wrists.

"Ow!" she cried when he tied it tight.

"Babe, we need to up your pain tolerance."

"I'm not sure I like the sound of that."

"You will."

He then tied her wrists to one of the slats in the headboard. Her boobs pressed into the bed, and she had to turn her head to the side to breathe well. She still had her panties around her knees. In her current position, she was ripe for some doggie-style fucking. But he wasn't done tending to her ass. He backhanded a posterior cheek.

"I want an apology. A proper apology."

He walloped the other buttock and stepped back to admire her ass. Despite the darkness of her skin, he could see it blush from the force of his blow.

"Shit. You ain't serious," she said.

He dipped his hand between her legs again and fondled her clit. It was hard to create any friction with all the wetness there, but he managed to strum the little nub with effect.

"Mmmmm," she moaned, spreading her legs a little wider.

He pulled back and slapped her ass again. "My apology, babe."

"I'm sorry," she grumbled into the bed.

He spanked her hard. "What was that?"

She yelped. "You don't have to hit so hard."

"I could do this all night."

It was half true. Her ass was luscious enough that spanking it was more fun than watching the '9ers on a Monday night. But he had such a hard-on right now, he wasn't going to hold out much longer. He smacked her so hard she nearly went into the headboard.

"Okay! Okay!" she gasped. "I'm sorry."

"I'm sorry, Sir," he corrected.

"I'm sorry, Sir."

"Good job."

He rubbed her sore bottom.

"Shit, you don't mess around, do you?" she breathed.

"Did you like it?"

She thought for a moment. "Depends how you finish this."

He slid his hand back between her thighs and stroked her.

"I like it," she purred.

He played with her engorged clit till she whimpered and writhed, pushing herself into his hand, wanting more. He could tell when he had hit a particularly sensitive spot when she cried out. It helped that she was vocal.

"Oh, baby," she cooed when he quickened his caress.

He loved hearing a woman about to come. Her sounds became more hurried, more shallow.

"Ask permission before you come," he reminded her.

When she didn't respond, he slowed his ministrations.

"May I come? Please, Sir?"

"Good girl."

Soon she was spasming against his hand, legs trembling, before sinking into the bed. She let out a contented sigh. He was tempted to rip off his underwear and take her, but he needed to make the experience more memorable. Looking around, he noticed the little tray of birth control pills on her bedside table.

"How often do you have sex?"

"Depends if I'm seeing anyone. It's not like I gotta pick up a guy every week. Not when I can do things for myself."

"Yeah? How often?"

"I usually come a couple times a day."

"How do you like to do it?"

"I got a mess of toys."

"Where?"

"Top drawer of the dresser."

She grunted when he left the bed to investigate.

"Rabbit ears, nice," he said, pulling out a long pink vibrator. "Good old Magic Wand. A regular dildo. A glass dildo. A double dildo. You do have a lot of toys, babe."

Taking out a particularly wide and long dildo, he whistled. "These could make a guy feel real inadequate."

"I don't use that one all that much."

He selected a simple battery-operated dildo. "Ready for round two?"

The shine in her eyes made him melt. Eagerly, he strode over to the bed and turned the vibrator on. She gave him a sultry look. *God, I got to fuck her soon.*

He rubbed the vibrator gently along her folds, then let it linger on her clit. She moaned in appreciation. Her orgasm loomed quickly. He pressed the vibrator more fully against her, then retracted.

"Argh," she grumbled. "I was so close!"

"I know. But you didn't ask for permission yet."

"Bastard," she said beneath her breath.

"I heard that."

He gave her nipple a playful tweak, then shed his underpants. Though his cock sprang free, the pressure in his groin remained strong as ever.

"I was wondering when you'd bring it out," she said. "Thought you were going shy on me."

He laughed. If it was one thing his cock wasn't, it was shy. She wiggled her butt. He groaned. It was the most perfect looking ass he had ever seen. Smooth, round, supple. He hoped she would let him take her ass at some point.

He rubbed his shaft along her folds. The heat and wetness made his blood boil with desire. He ground the tip of his cock against her.

"Fuck me already," she groaned, trying to impale herself on him.

Putting a hand on her back, he held her off. "Ask for it nicely."

"Fuck me already. Please. Sir."

Thank God. He aimed himself at her slit and pushed the crown of his penis inside. Her molten pussy grabbed at him. *Holy mother of...*

He closed his eyes and tried not to let her exquisiteness overwhelm him. He took a few fortifying breaths. When he was sure he had himself under control, he pushed his cock further. Her muscles flexed around him, impatient to have more of him inside of her. *Nice and easy,* he told himself. He didn't usually have to worry about control, but maybe because he had been lusting after Charlene for so long, the anticipation was too great. She made another move to encase the whole of his cock. He slapped a buttock to remind her of her place. At a leisurely pace, he slid the remainder of his erection inside. This was heaven. With his cock buried inside her pulsing, wet heat, her ass nestled against his pelvis.

After several moments, he began a slow and deliberate thrust, dragging his cock along her most sensitive spot. She shivered. He could tell she was impatient, but she allowed him to dictate the pace. Gradually, he quickened his motions, driving a little harder, a little deeper, each time.

"Oh, yes," she approved.

She met each thrust, her pussy pushing against him. Soon they had created a rhythm that had her panting and moaning her towards orgasm. But he slowed to a halt before she could reach the apex.

Remembering, she asked, "May I come, Sir?"

He resumed his thrusting, loving the way his pelvis slammed into her ass. He held onto her hips so that he could ensure his cock penetrated her at the optimal angle.

"May I come? May I come?" she gasped with urgency.

"You may."

With a cry, she exploded, her body jerking against the bonds. After several shudders and tremors, she would have buckled at the knees if he hadn't held onto her hips. Still inside of her, his cock throbbed a few times. When her climax had completely passed, he propped himself over her with one arm and reached for the vibrator with the other. Clicking it on to its medium setting, he held it to her clitoris.

"Oh, God! I'm gonna come!" she gasped within minutes.

He rolled his hips into her. "Ask for it."

"M-May I come, Sir?"

"Not yet."

"P-Please. I'm gonna c-come."

"Hold it."

"I c-can't!"

With a wail, she erupted again. This time, he pounded his cock into her for his own benefit, bucking against her several times until he shot his load in glorious conclusion. His body shuddered from head to toe. Only when the last of his orgasm had been pumped from him did he realize she was grimacing, her clit too sensitive for the vibrator. He quickly switched it off and withdrew. She sank into the bed, her legs stretched out, her panties still around her knees.

"That was good," she murmured. "Thank you, Sir."

Lying beside her, he smiled. She wasn't such a bad student, after all. He wasn't much for teaching, never wanted to be a teacher's assistant though he had been asked once by one of the hotter female professors, but he didn't mind taking on Charlene.

He massaged her scalp through her hair. "Ready for round three?"

"Round three? I'm hungry now. Can we order Mongolian beef?"

"Oh no. You don't get to eat yet. You came without permission."

She frowned, looking almost like a little girl who had been told she couldn't have her chocolate chip cookie yet.

"We're going to do this until you get it right."

He stroked his cock. It would be ready to go again shortly. He pulled her panties off and flipped her onto her back. Rolling onto her, he began kissing his way from her neck down to her belly button while caressing her with his hands.

"I'm serious. I'm really hungry. Can't we pick up round three after dinner?"

He couldn't decide if he was glad that her last orgasm had been so satisfying that she was done or that it wasn't good enough to top her appetite for food. He switched the vibrator on again. It was glistening with her juices. He circled it around her nipples, then trailed it down her torso, across her pelvis, and back to her clit.

"Wait—"

Her clit was still a little too sensitive, but he kept it there anyway. She squirmed and tried to buck her hips away from the vibration. He put a hand to her groin to hold her in place, then clicked the vibrator to the high setting.

"Shit!" she squealed.

She jerked her limbs and squeezed her eyes shut. He found a part of her clitoris that was less jarring. Eventually the uncomfortable sensitivity melded into pleasure. She moaned and her body arched. She was beginning to scale another orgasm.

"Not yet," he said.

"Please, please, please, please."

"No."

She inhaled sharply and dug her fingers into her palms.

"*Please,*" she pleaded.

"Almost."

But she couldn't hold it. Her eyes rolled into the back of the head and her body went into another paroxysm. He reduced the vibrator to its lowest setting. She shivered violently several times. She was so damn sexy when she came.

He tossed the vibrator aside. His cock was hard again.

"Sorry," she mumbled.

He smiled. "That's okay. We have all night to practice."

Her eyes widened. "I got work in the morning."

"Then you better get it right sooner rather than later."

"I'm gonna kill you, wh—"

He put a finger on her lips. "Unh unh."

She glared at him and pulled at her bonds. Ignoring her frustration, he slid down and positioned himself between her legs. *Holy shit.* It wasn't just a puddle here, it was a pond. He decided he wanted her even more wet. He enclosed his mouth around her clitoris and licked. Her hips bucked at his touch but she soon settled down. He licked her a little more, then sucked on the bud. Her moisture coated his lower face, but he liked the musk of her desire. When she began to respond positively to him, he inserted two fingers into her vagina and petted the raised area inside.

"Oh!" she gasped in delight.

His fingers caressed the spot over and over. He reached his other hand to fondle a breast. It took her a little longer to near her climax this time, but he was patient. He wanted to see her squirt. He pumped his hand more vehemently against her pussy. She moaned and mewed, her face glowing with the impending orgasm.

"May I come?" she murmured. "May I come, Sir?"

He didn't think he would ever tire of hearing her say those words.

"Not yet."

"Please."

"You can do this."

Her fingers and toes clenched.

"You can do this," he repeated as he increased his assault on her G-spot.

She whined but held on.

"Now. Come for me, babe."

A gush of liquid streamed from her. He pushed his hand deeper into her, causing another stream to cascade from her.

Holy fuck.

"Thank you, Sir," she panted.

"Round five is for me."

He picked up her ankles and held them high in one hand. She was flexible enough that he had easy access to her cunt. Holding her hips off the bed by her ankles, he shoved his cock into her. Having come already, his stamina was improved the second time around. And he pumped himself long and hard. Her body eventually joined him on her own journey. Seeing the promise of another orgasm for her, he held on. He put her legs down on each shoulder and increased the force of his pommeling. He could tell she liked it hard. Her body felt so beautiful and strong beneath his.

"Do I—do I have permission—?"

"Anytime, babe."

Together they bucked until they came in near unison. With a roar, his seed filled her, and he felt another coat of her moisture mingle with his. Rolling off her, he untied her wrists and pulled her against his sweaty body. She nestled her head against the crook of his arm and sighed.

"Thank you, Sir."

15

Earth to Charlene."

Audrey waved a hand in front of her friend, who was staring into the corner of her computer monitor.

Charlene looked up. "Hunh?"

Leaning on the counter of the reception area, Audrey took a closer look at Charlene. "What's the matter? Didn't you get enough sleep last night?"

Charlene shifted in her seat. "No. And I didn't get my caramel mocha this morning."

"Seriously?"

"Ran late," Charlene grumbled.

"I'll watch the desk for you if you want to go grab something now."

"Nah. I had a cup of coffee from the break room. It doesn't have the same mojo, though."

"I need a large conference room for my meeting with the joint powers authority. The city and the county are sending people—is that a bag of carrots?"

Audrey stared in disbelief at the orange vegetables on Charlene's desk. One of them actually looked half eaten. Those couldn't be Charlene's, but then what would she be doing with a bag of carrots?

"Oh, yeah, I needed something to munch on to keep me awake."

"Where's the cheese danish?"

"Trying to go healthy."

Audrey blinked. "Say what?"

"Well, I don't need those empty calories."

Audrey stared. "Who are you and what did you do with my friend Charlene?"

Charlene rolled her eyes. "What? Is eating healthy so freaky?"

"It is when you do it."

Charlene pursed her lips and lowered her voice. "Fine. Blaine's making me do it."

"Blaine is making you do it," Audrey repeated as if she were trying out a foreign language. "I don't get it."

"I think if I impress him enough, he might take me to The French Laundry."

"I thought you already got him to take you to Ballander's."

"I'm gettin' greedy."

"But why do you have to impress him first?"

Charlene waved her hand dismissively. "Long story."

Audrey eyed her friend skeptically. "Un-hunh."

"We're just messin' around."

"You're messin' around with Blaine? Guess I shouldn't be surprised." Audrey grinned. "You both being sluts and all."

"Right? Right!"

"But what's that got to do with you eating carrots?"

"What? You never seen me eat vegetables before?"

"I've seen you eat a salad when it was covered with sirloin strips and blue cheese dressing. But those are just plain old carrots."

Charlene gave up. "Okay, okay. Blaine and I playing with a little bondage and domination."

Audrey raised an eyebrow.

"He says I got to eat this crap," Charlene continued. "The boy threw out my frozen pot pies. Said the sodium count in those things would take out a lineman. Stocked my fridge with this shit."

Audrey stared in disbelief. "Holy shit. Blaine did that?"

"Yeah, I'm not so sure I can last much longer. Sex is good, though."

"How long has he been making you eat healthy?"

"We just started yesterday. But, honest, I'm gonna go crazy. I could kill someone. Which would be bad. So if I went downstairs and got me a chocolate chip muffin, I would be doing the world a whole lotta good."

"What happens if you don't eat healthy?"

Charlene shrugged. "I don't get my chance to dine at The French Laundry. But what he doesn't know won't hurt him."

Charlene had a mischievous gleam in her eyes, and Audrey knew the chocolate chip muffin had won out over the carrots.

"Never thought I'd be saying this," Audrey started, "but maybe you hooking up with Blaine is not a bad thing. Didn't know he was into healthy living."

"Would you believe he made fun of my apartment?"

"He did?"

"Said, between the frozen pizza and the mess, I lived like a child."

"Your place is messy."

Charlene glared at her. "Whose side you on, girl?"

"Charlene was eating *what?*" the perky Korean-American girl with the short spiky hair asked Audrey as they sorted through their clothes in one of the neighborhood laundromats in Russian Hill.

"Raw carrots," Audrey replied.

Having moved her clothes into the dryer, Audrey sat down and looked around to see who else was in the laundromat. It was almost as if she were looking for Rance, though she knew he wouldn't be frequenting this laundromat as he no longer lived in the neighborhood. It was crazy to think that they had actually been neighbors, given that he could have lived anywhere he wanted. And it was at this laundromat where she had dropped the gift card Charlene had given her as a Christmas gift. A gift card to an escort service, Pleasant Company. Except it wasn't exactly an escort service. More like a free sex service. She had dropped the card and Rance had picked it up to hand it back to her. According to Rance, he had looked up Pleasant Company when he got back to his apartment.

Thanks to the thin walls of the building, he had subsequently overheard her calling the company. And that was how they had gotten their start.

Maybe it was a bad sign that their relationship had begun with him posing as a gigolo.

"I don't believe it," Jan said, shaking her head.

"You know our girl," Audrey replied. "Guess she'll go to great lengths for great sex."

"But eating vegetables? Blaine must be really good in bed."

"Yeah. I don't really want to think about it."

"That's supposed to be my line."

The little bell above the laundromat chimed, and they both turned their heads. A slender, beautiful brunette with long straight hair fumbled with her overloaded laundry basket as she tried to push aside the heavy door. Jan rushed over.

"Where's Izzy?" Audrey asked when Jan jogged back after helping the young woman.

"She's staying with her folks down in San Jose so they can hit the local flower markets in the morning. I hope she doesn't go crazy. I mean, I would've been fine with getting married at City Hall. It's a pretty majestic place. And it's historic. It's where the first gay couple in California were married."

"Well, Izzy is a romantic."

"I think City Hall is romantic. A lot cheaper, too. Romance shouldn't cost hundreds of dollars. It's pretty crazy how much people spend on a single party. If you think about it, it doesn't make much financial sense, especially since so many people get divorced anyway. All that money down the drain."

"You and Izzy have a budget, though, right?"

"Sure. I agreed to a bigger wedding because Izzy said it meant a lot to her family, and you know it took her family a while to get used to the idea of her being lesbian. And I know she'd have fun being a bride, but did you see the price tag on that wedding dress? It's five times what I'm paying to rent a tuxedo!"

"She gets to keep the dress."

"For what? So she can wear it if she gets married again? Brides should rent their dresses. That's what they do in Asia. No one except rich people shell out that kind of money for a dress they're only going to wear once in their life."

"You can hand it down to your daughter or granddaughter."

Jan rolled her eyes. "If we have a daughter. And if she'd want to wear a dress her mom wore decades ago. It's so impractical. I mean, it's not like either of us make a ton of money. Izzy might make more if she gets her CPA certification, but I can only make so much as a graphic designer. And we live in the most expensive place in the country. And she wants kids. Do you know how much childcare costs in San Francisco? We're probably going to have to move out to the suburbs for childcare and good schools. And I don't want to move out of the city."

"Whoa, Nellie. You're getting way ahead of yourself."

Jan took a deep breath. "I guess. But didn't you ever find yourself thinking ahead when you were with Rance?"

Audrey didn't answer because she was guilty as charged. She had fantasized about marrying Rance but also foresaw them getting into disagreements because that had already happened. Marriage meant more pain if those disagreements didn't get resolved.

"Yeah, but you and Izzy are different," Audrey replied. "You've been sweethearts for a long time. And Rance and I don't have enough in common. And don't tell me we had each other in common."

"Hell, no. I leave that corny stuff to Izzy. But I thought you guys did have a lot in common in your values and openness. Your sense of humor."

"I meant in terms of our background. There has to be enough there for a relationship to work out, unless you're some shallow gold-digger willing to give up a part of who you are. It's idealistic to think otherwise."

"You really believe that or you wanna believe that?"

Audrey didn't answer. It was too late in the evening for her to answer a question like that. And she had a stack of budget analyses to pour through.

Standing on the balcony of his room at the *sur Mer* with a glass of zinfandel in hand, Rance listened to the sound of the Pacific. It was a much different ocean from the Atlantic. To him, it could be more moody, the waves larger and more imposing, but it was no less beautiful.

His mind drifted back to the first time he'd brought Audrey to the hotel. It always surprised him how vividly he remembered their moments together. The sex had been great, the conversations great. The combination of the two were great...

"What do *you* do for fun?" Audrey had returned.

It was their first evening together in the penthouse suite. They were wearing matching hotel robes.

"Wait, I know. Seducing women in posh hotel rooms," she had answered for herself.

"That and squash."

"Come again?"

"Squash."

"You get kinky with vegetables?"

This time his laughter was a long continuous rumble. "It's a sport, somewhat like racquet ball. A lot of fun. We should try it sometime."

"I don't know. I'm not exactly the sporting type."

"Oh, I think you are. Come here."

He waited until Audrey realized he was being serious. She got up and strode over to him. He unwrapped his robe to reveal his cock, hard and stiff as a flagpole. Taking her by the hand, he pulled her down to him. Wrapping his free hand behind her neck, he brought her mouth to his, their tongues melding. Without letting go of her lips, he grabbed her ass and pulled her to him until she was straddled over his legs. He unwrapped the sash that held her robe in place and pulled open the garment to reveal her breasts. With her kneeling on the chair, her breasts were at the perfect height for his mouth. He pushed the two orbs together, then sucked greedily at one nipple, pulling at it until it was as stiff and pointed as his cock. He put a finger to her clitoris. Tugged it, fondled it. Then he slipped the finger into her wetness. Her vagina grabbed at his finger hungrily. He pushed another finger up into her and rubbed a part of her front vaginal walls. She responded with receptive moaning and uneven breaths. Her lashes fluttered.

And then he pressed his thumb onto her clitoris while the other two digits remained buried inside her. He worked his thumb and fingers simultaneously, massaging her in her most intimate places. Just as the waves of pleasure were about to crest for her, he pulled out of her. He reached into the pocket of his robe and pulled out a condom. He tore it open with his teeth and rolled it down his penis.

"It's all you," he told her, lifting her by the hips and settling her onto his cock.

She moaned as his hard member slid into her. She shifted on top of him in order to feel him from all angles. She rolled her hips around.

"Oh, baby," he groaned and brought her head to his, crushing her lips with his.

After a long wet kiss, she pulled away from him in order to sit more squarely on top of him. She pushed herself up off his cock slightly, then dropped herself down. Up, then down again, and up and down. Rance groaned again and settled back into the cushions of the chair. He cupped her breasts with both hands. Audrey pistoned her body up and down his shaft, quickening the motion as her need spread like wildfire through her veins. Her breasts bounced, her butt cheeks slapped against his thighs.

She bounded up and down his body, rutting against him as hard as she could, trying to drive his cock harder against her clit, deeper inside her. Perspiration began culminating between her breasts and at her nose. Now hot and sweaty, she shed her robe.

"Damn, this is almost as hard as that stair climbing machine," she muttered.

But every time she considered slowing down, he would either buck his hips against her or circle his thumb on her clitoris enough to make her push ahead towards that much-desired climax. And when she finally reached it, her body broke into convulsions until, awash with relief, she collapsed on top of him. She lay against him as if she might fall asleep. He stroked her hair while his cock, still hard, pulsed inside of her.

"You didn't come," she said, lifting her head to look into his eyes.

"Oh, we're not done," he answered. "What's Christmas without presents?"

16

What's wrong with eating a salad?" Charlene demanded as Blaine drove his car up Jones Street in Russian Hill. "I thought salads were hella healthy."

"Not if you drown it in dressing. You might as well have a hamburger," he replied.

She narrowed her eyes at him. The smart-ass had a response for everything.

"Well, I'm craving a hamburger after eating a boring old salad for lunch," she huffed, looking out the window at the different restaurants and businesses. Although the pasta dish he had made for her the other night was decent, she hoped they were going out for dinner tonight. She was dressed for it. Sporting five-inch platform pumps and a wrap-around dress with a low V-neck, she knew she looked hot. At the office, she had worn a camisole underneath. But now that she was off work, she had removed the camisole and let her cleavage show in all its glory. Even smooth Mr. Blaine Edwards had nearly stumbled when she had removed her coat to get in the car.

"I like the look of that restaurant," she said of the corner restaurant as they sat at a red light. She admired the water feature inside. "Looks pretty happening, and I could do with some fusion cuisine. I know they say you can't judge a book by its cover an' all, but I like pretty restaurants."

"The ambience is part of the experience," Blaine agreed.

Charlene watched sadly as they drove away.

"Not that I don't like a hole-in-the-wall type of restaurant, like in Chinatown or the Mission—before it got so gentrified," Blaine continued, "but that's really more Rance's style when he goes out to eat. I'd take Ballander's any day."

"So where we gonna eat then? You're not planning to cook again, are you?"

"Ouch."

Ignoring his wounded look, she rolled her eyes. "I'm not saying you're a bad cook. You're better than me, I'll give you that. But...well, you know."

"You eat frozen shit."

"What are you? Some kind of food snob?"

"Look, I used to subsist on that stuff, too. Hell, I used to buy instant noodle in bulk. But that kind of processed food is loaded with sodium and all kinds of crap."

She folded her arms. "If I had your kind of money, believe me, I wouldn't be living on frozen pot pies and TV dinners."

Blaine was silent, surprising her with his lack of a comeback.

"What? You don't like me pointing out you're rich?" she prompted.

"No, no. It's just—I got asked to sponsor this food summit at Stanford. I attended one of the panels. A lot of people can't afford to eat healthy in this country, which then leads to all kinds of health issues they're ill-equipped to deal with financially. It's an ugly cycle. It's sad and it's wrong."

She raised her brows. Was he serious or just trying to impress her with his compassion?

"Guess it's nice that a rich kid school can at least talk about how the other half lives," she said, though she didn't completely buy it.

"The other ninety percent. And Stanford isn't a rich kid's university, though I lived a pretty sheltered life, I'll admit. Didn't really think much about the greater community till I got to Stanford. There was this really hot activist chick. Had to join one of those student hunger strikes to impress her. Don't think I even knew what we were striking for. Something about better working conditions for grape-pickers, I think."

His levity had returned, and she couldn't help but smile.

"You care so much about the other ninety percent, then why don't you take me out to dinner?" she asked with charm.

He looked over at her. “Sure, babe. If you’ve been a good girl.”

“I ate a salad for lunch, didn’t I?”

Blaine pulled into a multi-storied residential building. She frowned.

“We walking to the restaurant?” she asked after they had parked and gotten out of the car.

“You’re just in this for a free meal, aren’t you?”

“Hey, white boy got himself some brains.”

Before she could take a step, he pinned her against the vehicle with his body.

“You’re asking for it to be rough,” he said.

The garage had suddenly become cramped and warm—really warm. Her breath became shallow.

“I’m sorry, Sir.”

She wasn’t sure where that had come from, but it had fallen from her lips right away. He tilted her chin up with his thumb, and her heart started hammering away.

“You know,” he said, his voice low and husky, “you can’t expect I’d take you to dinner first when you’re looking this damn sexy.”

Emboldened by his compliment, she replied, “You want to get it on *before* dinner? You want to get to first base, you got to buy me dinner first.”

“Didn’t know you were so old-fashioned. Thought you were an enlightened sex fiend.”

“I am. *After* dinner,” she resisted.

“We did it first yesterday.”

“I was going easy on you.”

“Glad we’re playing by my rules then.”

His mouth was an inch from hers, and she was ready to capitulate. The area beneath her belly had come alive and maybe she wasn't as hungry for food as she was a few minutes ago. But when another car pulled into the garage, Blaine eased himself away. Taking her by the hand, he led her to the elevator. She supposed a little making out before dinner wouldn't be such a bad thing. Once inside the elevator, he pushed the button for the top floor and barely waited for the doors to close before he had her against the wall. Her legs weakened at the way his gaze devoured her. Strange how much hotter he had grown in her eyes. It wasn't that she didn't think he was good looking before, but now that he was up and close and personal—*very personal*—she appreciated his irises of crushed sapphire and even the way his blond locks fell across his forehead. He must've had a business meeting because he wore slacks and a matching grey blazer over his buttoned shirt, and he looked sexy all dressed up. He hovered over her, his body a hair from touching her in so many places. She could easily arch her back and make her breasts touch his chest. The guy definitely knew the art of anticipation, and the air crackled with tension.

"Have you been a good girl?" he asked, brushing aside a tendril of hair from her face.

He had one hand against the elevator wall, right next to her waist. It wouldn't take much for him to grab an ass cheek.

Grab me, grope me, her body screamed.

"Depends what you mean by 'good girl,'" she replied, her voice breathy. There was barely any air between them.

"Did you do what I told you?"

"Sure. And I ate your damn carrots, too. Most of 'em. Half of 'em."

He cocked his head and looked at her as if she were some kid that was explaining how the dog ate her homework. Leaning in, he whispered into her ear, "What else?"

She shivered. "Coffee. You can't expect a girl to give up caffeine."

"You're leaving something out, babe. What else did you have?"

Her heartbeat quickened, and not completely from her rising lust.

"Wh-what do you mean?"

Cupping her chin between his thumb and forefinger, he tilted her gaze up toward him. "You had something else from the café downstairs."

"What? You spying on me now?" she responded defensively. "You got a webcam at my desk?"

"No. But people don't forget babes as hot as you. I passed by your building and stopped in the café to ask if the cashier remembered a super-sexy black woman coming in. He remembered exactly what you bought: a chocolate cream-cheese muffin."

She didn't know whether to stoke her anger that he had checked up on her or let it slide in favor of the arousal still heating up inside of her. She decided on the former and knocked his hand away. With a ding, the elevator doors opened. She walked out in a huff and went to stand in front of his door. Damn asshole hadn't trusted her. Nevermind that he was right not to, but she wasn't sure she could let him make it to first base now. Stupid son of a bitch. And she was feeling super horny, too.

"You don't follow orders well, do you, babe?"

Arms folded, she didn't bother turning around to look at him. She needed to figure out how she was gonna handle this.

"Open the door," she muttered, then gasped when he came up behind her and pinned her to the door. This time his body pressed into her. She braced herself to keep from getting completely smushed into the door.

"You know what happens when you disobey."

Her mouth went dry but another part of her had started to get wet, really wet. He pushed his pelvis into her, and she moaned. Maybe if she got him all worked up, he'd forget about doing anything with her disobedience. She moved her ass against him. He brushed aside her hair to kiss and mouth her neck. She purred her approval, groaning when one of his hands cupped her breast and kneaded its fullness. She writhed between him and the door. He pressed his body harder against her.

"You ready for this?" he asked.

"Just open the damn door," she murmured, closing her eyes to contain the delicious agitation from overwhelming her.

"I would. But this isn't my door."

Her eyes flew open. "What?"

"My unit's around the corner."

She pushed herself away. He stepped away, allowing her room. She straightened her dress.

Blaine grinned. "I don't think Paul will mind us grinding against his door. He's a bit of a whore himself."

She tossed her hair. "Is he hot? Should we invite him into a threesome?"

"Being gay, he'd probably want to bang me more than you. And even if he weren't, I'm not ready to share."

He pulled her into him. She bumped into his very obvious, very hard erection. Another wave of heat washed over her as she pictured Blaine naked with another man.

"I don't mind watching," she said.

"You serious?"

She put her hands on his chest. "Why not? Men get off on the idea of two women making out. You never wondered what it would be like to fuck another man?"

"Wondered, sure. Don't know if I could actually do it."

She threaded her fingers through his hair and lifted a leg between his, running her knee along the inside of his leg. "Too bad. I could get off good watching two hard bodies doin' the nasty."

"Would I be pitching or catching?"

"Doesn't matter."

He lowered his head and took her mouth possessively in his. In seconds he had her slammed against the door again. He knew just the right amount of force to use, made it just rough enough to be arousing and not jarring. He devoured her with his mouth, and for a moment she wondered if he was actually going to fuck her against his neighbor's door.

Lust had reached a level for her where she would've been game to do it. She craned her neck. Desire swelled in her groin when he took mouthfuls of her throat as he thrust at her through their clothes.

"Paul wouldn't mind our little sex show in front of his place?" she murmured when he lowered his head and kissed her cleavage.

Blaine grabbed her buttock and squeezed. "You're not getting any that easy."

"Huh?"

Abruptly, he threw her over his shoulder and carried her down the hall. He fished out his keys and didn't set her down till they were inside his condo. She gasped at the view of the city laid out before the wall-to-wall windows. To their right was a chef's kitchen with a bar opening up to the living room. Unlike her apartment, his place was immaculately clean. He must have a housekeeping service, she figured. She walked over to the windows and looked over all the twinkling lights at her feet.

"Wow," she said.

Taking off his blazer, he went to the bar and poured her a rum and Coke. Not bad, she thought to herself. He knew her drink.

"The city's a lot like you," he said, standing next to her. "Gorgeous from every angle."

"You sweet talk all your subs?"

"I haven't had a sub in years."

"Oh. I'm special."

"You don't need me to say it. You know you are."

They clinked glasses and drank.

"You remember the rules?" he asked.

"Shit. This a test?"

"Sure. Remember them?"

"Hell no. I didn't know you were going to test me on them."

"You're a terrible student."

"Yeah, but you know I got A's from all the male teachers anyway."

"You do good in my class, you'll get more than an A."

She edged closer to him. "I like the sound of that."

"Rules. What are they?"

She rolled her eyes. "Umm, don't call you 'white boy'?"

"That was a command but not a rule."

"What's the difference?"

"Rule number one: you call me 'Sir.' You haven't been doing that, and I've let a lot of things slide."

She finished off her drink and ran a finger down his chest. "So spank me, Sir."

"Oh, I will."

"Do it now. The sooner you spank me, the sooner we can fuck."

She looked into his eyes and saw the effect she had on him. His eyes had dilated further and his jaw hardened. He took her empty glass and set both their glasses on the grand piano beside him.

"You play?" she asked.

"No. It came with the condo. I got no musical talents whatsoever."

"That's okay. You got other assets. Sir."

Feeling aggressive, she put a hand to his crotch and squeezed. The more she aroused him, the sooner they could get to the good stuff. He took her hand and replaced it by her side.

"Rule number two: you thank me for everything."

"Yes, Sir."

She groped his crotch again. He grabbed her wrist, twisted her arm around her back and bent her over the back of his white leather sofa.

"Three: you ask permission."

He spanked her hard. She yelped, surprised at the force of it.

"That hurt!" she exclaimed.

"Remember the rules next time," he replied, still holding her against the sofa. "Let's review. What's rule number one?"

"Uhhh...call you 'Sir.'"

"Very good. Number two?"

Crap. What was number two? Something a little strange. She racked her brain, then cried out again when he landed another hard smack on her ass.

"Ask permission?" she guessed. Despite the plushness of the sofa cushions, hers was not a comfortable position to be in.

"That's number three."

He pulled her dress up over ass, exposing her black lace thong and butt cheeks. He palmed one supple orb before whacking it.

"Ugh. I don't remember."

Smack!

"Do what you tell me," she tried.

"That's a given."

Smack!

Her backside burned. Good thing she wasn't a skinny, boney white chick and had some padding back there.

"Your ass is so fuckin' hot," he grumbled before walloping her some more.

She struggled against the sofa. "Shit! That's enough."

"Tell me what rule number two is."

He backhanded her arse.

She groaned. "I don't remember."

"Thank your master."

Oh right.

"So where's my thanks?"

He slapped her more gently this time, but she got the threat.

"Thank you, thank you, thank you."

His hand bit into her flesh once more.

"Mother fucker, what was that for?"

"Sir," he reminded her.

"Thank you, Sir," she mumbled.

Her ass was on fire—and so was her pussy. She could feel it on her heat-soaked thong. He caressed her smarting buttocks and ran a finger along the edge of her thong.

"I want to fuck this ass so bad," he said, rubbing her folds through the flimsy fabric.

Her legs quivered at the surge of pleasure between her thighs, overpowering the smarting of her ass. He reached around her hip and stroked her clit. His fingers felt soooo good, hitting just the right spot. Oh, baby, she was ready to come. He just had to keep it up a little longer.

But of course he didn't. Slowly, he withdrew his fingers. She nearly whimpered at the loss.

"You gotta ask for it," he explained. "Rule number three."

Damn rules, she wanted to say. Instead, she grumbled, "Thank you for reminding me, Sir."

He gave her ass a pat before letting her up from the sofa. "You're welcome."

"I need a drink."

He raised his brows.

She rolled her eyes. "Sir, may I have a drink?"

"Better. When was the last time you ate?"

"Three-ish."

"You shouldn't drink too much on an empty stomach."

"Well, whose fault is that?"

"I don't want you too drunk. You'll miss out on all the fun."

"Fun?" she scoffed, folding her arms. "For you."

He bridged the distance between them, his eyes gleaming as he looked down at her. "It's all about you, babe."

"This 'babe' is ready to get it on."

"If you hadn't disobeyed me and gotten that muffin, you'd be on your second orgasm by now. Follow orders next time."

Turning, he retrieved the glasses from the piano and went back to the bar. At that moment, she couldn't decide if she wanted to wring his neck more than she wanted to fuck him. Her gaze fell to his ass. Okay, she still wanted to fuck him more than anything. She followed him to the bar.

"So I've been a bad little girl," she purred as he refilled her drink halfway. "I deserved the spanking."

"The spanking was for forgetting the rules. Your punishment for the muffin hasn't even started."

She frowned as she took her drink from him. He filled his glass with some fancy brand of water and clinked glasses.

"Cheers, babe."

"So what is my punishment?"

"You'll see. Do you remember your safety word?"

"Why? Am I gonna need it?"

"What's the safety word?"

She had to think about it before coming up with the answer. "Cotton candy."

He wrapped an arm around her waist and pulled her close. "Good. Then we can get started."

Setting aside his glass, he swept her into his arms and carried her into the bedroom. Though she was a little concerned about what her punishment entailed, she was also excited. At least now they were getting somewhere.

"Nice," she said when she saw that the bedroom had wall-to-wall windows showing off the same spectacular view.

He slid the switch to a dim setting, and she turned her attention to the king-sized four-post bed in the center of the room. It had nice white bedding. Not too bachelor. He set her down and started kissing her. Her body responded immediately, and she had to agree with his assessment of drinking too much. She was on a high already, and she didn't want alcohol to slow down her orgasm in any way. Returning to her previous plan of seducing him so that he couldn't carry out or had to minimize his intended punishment, she kissed him hard, diving her tongue into his mouth. She rubbed his erection with her body, then palmed one of his buttocks through his slacks. He untied her dress and unwrapped the front of it. She took in a deep breath to expand her chest. She could see the appreciation in his eyes as he scanned her black balconet bra. He kissed the top of one boob. Leaning against the dresser, she let her head fall back to allow him full access. With his lips, he caressed the area of her collarbone and the tops of her breasts. After he had seared several kisses all over her chest, she reached for his shirt and tore it open, buttons flying.

He paused. "This is one of my favorite shirts."

"You can afford more," she dismissed as she kissed and sucked at his neck while her hands ran greedily over his undershirt, which was cut like a tank top.

"And you didn't ask permission first."

"My bad."

She licked and nipped at his nipples through the undershirt as she undid the rest of the buttons on his shirt.

"I like a woman who goes after what she wants," he contemplated aloud, "but right now, you're a piss-poor sub."

Impatient, she pushed up his undershirt to access his chest. She ran her lips hungrily over his pecs before locking onto a nipple. She sucked until he groaned.

"That's enough," he groaned.

She sucked harder.

"I said enough."

Fisting his hand in her hair, he pulled hard. She gasped, releasing his nipple from her mouth.

"If we're going to do this, we're not going to half-ass it," he said. "You're already getting way too much leeway. Now take the dress off."

Happy to show off her figure even more, she slid out of the dress. She would have liked him to be at least as undressed as she, but he looked plenty hot in his mussed-up shirt. He eyed her from head to toe with appreciation and stepped to her, fitting his body against hers. She thought he was going to start kissing her again, but he reached for the top drawer of the dresser behind her. Pulling out the drawer, he retrieved a cord of rope. With a quick arm around her, he whipped her off the dresser and toward the bed. Now he began kissing her again. She ground herself against him, ready for more than just kissing. She felt the post of the bed against her back. At least they were getting closer. He pulled her arms overhead as their tongues dueled. She held onto the post behind with both hands.

"Good," he murmured against her lips. "Now we can take care of business."

"Business?"

Unwinding the rope, he wrapped it around her wrists, tying her hands to the post of the bed.

"I like rope play," she cooed.

When he was done, she tested the security of her bindings. He had tied it tight. She definitely wasn't going anywhere.

"I'll be right back," he said. "Stay there, ok?"

"Very funny."

While he was gone, she looked around and saw herself reflected in the windows. *Damn, I look hot tied to this bedpost.* She didn't have a lot of body hair to begin with and only needed a little waxing around the pubic hair. Her body was lean in all the right places, smooth in the belly and limbs, and full in the bust and hips. Wearing only her heels and lingerie, she would have felt cool but for the desire burning all over her. She arched her back and writhed against the bedpost. Preoccupied with how she looked in the window, she hadn't seen him reenter.

"Ever wish you had a double so you could fuck yourself?" he asked from the threshold, holding his drink.

"That's just weird...babe. Sir."

She struggled against her bonds for show, parting her thick lips and panting a little. She rolled her hips, then rubbed her backside along the post. The glazed look in his eyes told her it was having the effect she wanted. She decided she would have made a pretty good pole dancer. He walked over to her, desire blazing in his eyes.

"You are way too hot to be legal," he said.

He touched the bottom of his glass to the swell of one breast. She gasped at the cold against her warm skin. Languidly, he ran the glass across the top of the breast. She looked into the contents of the glass.

"You're a light drinker?" she inquired.

"Given what I plan to do, it would be irresponsible of me to drink too much."

A shiver went up her spine. She suddenly felt very helpless. What if he did things that she didn't like? She had the safety word—what was it again? Popcorn? No. Cotton Candy. That was it. But still, she wouldn't know to use the word until after he started, right? She didn't want to be seen as a chicken.

Swallowing, she asked breathlessly, "What do you plan to do?"

"For me to know and you to find out."

He trailed the glass between her boobs and down the center of her torso. She let out a haggard breath. The ice in the water had caused condensation on the outside of the glass. The faint dampness transferred to her body. The glass traveled past her belly button and across her midsection. She licked her lips.

"Well, whatever you do, I hope it doesn't take too long before you fuck me."

"Who says you're getting fucked? You haven't exactly been a good girl."

She frowned. He was kidding, right? Of course they were going to have sex. That's what they were here for. There was no way he could resist fucking her.

His drink came to rest against her thigh.

"You know you want a piece of this," she said, wiggling seductively.

He gripped her hip. "And I intend to take it. All of it."

She held his smoldering stare. "Then let's get it on. Sir."

Releasing her, he set his glass on the dresser and removed his shirt. *Yum*, she thought to herself as she eyed his sculpted arms and how his undershirt stretched across his chest. Opening a drawer, he pulled out a cordless Magic Wand.

"You keep a vibrator?" she asked.

He smiled and the way his eyes twinkled made her melt. A little.

"Believe it or not, I use this to massage my back muscles, but I like its other purpose better." He turned it on low. "It's up to you to hold it in place."

He nestled it between her legs and pressed the head of the massager against her mound. She closed her eyes and sighed at the familiar and pleasurable vibrations, but it wasn't as easy as she thought to keep it in place. She had to clench her thighs pretty good.

"Mmmm. Thank you, Sir," she said.

He raised his brows. "Good girl.'

Strange, but she felt giddy at the compliment, like a student getting praised by her teacher.

"You can turn it higher, you know," she said. "Sir."

"You gotta earn that, babe."

Back at the dresser, he pulled out a flogger. She was pretty sure it was called a cat o' nine tails.

"Damn," she breathed. "You're more into this shit than I thought."

He unfurled the flogger and let the tails dangle to the floor.

"Remember the safety word?"

She gulped and hesitated. He whipped the flogger in the air. It made a snapping sound.

"Cotton candy!" she exclaimed.

Lightly, he aimed the flogger at her thigh. She jumped, mostly in surprise. The wand dropped to the floor.

"You got to do better than that," he said. "I'm not going to be picking this thing up all night."

Retrieving it, he placed it back between her thighs.

"Sorry," she mumbled. "I've never been flogged before."

"Don't worry. I'll take it easy till you can handle more."

He allowed her some time to get reacquainted with the vibrations. She couldn't wait for him to turn it higher. Gently, he lapped the tails of the flogger against her leg. Gradually, he increased his force, and when he actually whipped the flogger, it wasn't so bad. He landed it several times on the outside of her thigh, and it actually felt like getting a massage. But when the tips of the tails hit her, it stung. Yelping, she accidentally relaxed her thigh muscles. The wand fell to the floor again.

"You said you were going to take it easy!"

He held the wand up to her. "You want this thing on high, don't you?"

She nodded.

"Then you got to start earning it. Next time you drop it, it's gone for good."

She pursed her lips, unsure she liked this game. But what could she do? She wanted to come.

"Want it?" he asked.

"Yes, Sir."

He placed the wand back, stepped back, and delivered a similar blow to her other thigh. This time she had braced herself and kept her thighs clenched against the precious vibrator.

"Where's my 'thank you'?"

"Thank you!"

"Sir."

"Sir!"

Jesus, why was there so much to remember?

He turned her to the side so that he could whip her ass. He laid off the tips of the tails this time, so there was less sting.

"Thank you, Sir."

By now the wand had gotten her nice and toasty and very wet between her legs. She desperately needed him to turn up the power. He landed the flogger in different parts of her body, including the sides of her breasts, making her whole body come alive. She made sure to thank him after each blow. Flogging wasn't as bad as she had feared.

"Good," he praised.

"Can I get it on high now, Sir?"

"Just remember that you can't come without permission."

He reached between her legs and flipped the switch. She cried out in glee. He adjusted the wand till it was snug against her folds.

"Ohhhh, thank you," she moaned, closing her eyes and leaning back against the bedpost. If she gave herself over, she could probably come in two minutes.

"I think you're ready for more."

Stepping back, he whipped the tip of the tails against her breast. Her eyes flew open and she nearly lost the wand. She stared at him. He waited.

"Thank you, Sir."

Pleased, he whipped her again, a little harder this time. Now it hurt.

"Th-thank you, Sir."

She clenched her thighs harder. No way she was going to lose the wand now. Not after she had earned it. She braced herself for the next blow. He flogged her legs, her breasts, and the side of her butt. She had gotten into a rhythm of thanking him after each lash, but the magic of the wand was reaching a fevered pitch and, between the sting of the flogger and the scintillating vibrations between her legs, she started to lose track. There was the oh-so-marvelous build-up of tension in her clit and groin contrasting with the bite of the nine-tails. She couldn't decide if she should gasp in pain or moan in pleasure. She felt ready to burst.

Suddenly, the wand was whipped away. She would have preferred to be hit in the gut. Her mouth agape, she stared at him, a little disoriented but mostly stunned.

"You were about to come before asking permission," he explained.

She groaned. She had been on the verge of coming, and she had been trying to hold off. But between that and bracing for the next strike and the thanking, she hadn't managed rule number three. Fucking rule number three. Her clit did not appreciate having the wand taken from it. Throbbing angrily, it wanted to finish. She rubbed her thighs together and clenched her pussy, but it didn't get her anywhere.

"May I please come, Sir?" she tried.

"Let's try something else," he said, turning off the wand.

She bit her tongue from saying something that would put her in more trouble. She did not like having her climax taken from her, but she was probably more upset at the fact that he seemed so calm and collected when he should be ripping her panties from her. She let out a wistful sigh as he put the wand on the dresser. He set the flogger beside it and opened the drawer, withdrawing two metal clamps attached to each other with a small link chain. He slipped them into his pocket and returned to her. He wedged two fingers between her thighs and felt her soaking thigh. When his fingers slid aside the fabric and grazed her clit, she started to tremble.

"Thank you, Sir."

He rubbed her engorged bud, slick from her wetness.

"Oh, that feels good. May I come now, Sir?"

"Not yet."

Retracting his fingers, he reached for the mesh and lace cups of her bra. He yanked them down and exposed her nipples. Cupping her breasts, he perused them in obvious appreciation and passed his thumbs over her nipples. They jutted out at him, a wanton bid for attention. Lowering his head, he captured one of the nipples in his mouth and lightly sucked. Lightning bolts oscillated between her nipples and the area between her thighs.

"Thank you, Sir. Suck them harder, Sir."

She arched herself into his mouth and started writhing when he dropped his hand back between her legs, fondling her through her panties.

"May I come, Sir?" she asked dutifully.

He nibbled on her nipple. "Not yet."

"Please, Sir..."

Damn. His fingers felt so good. She'd prefer his cock, but coming this way was good, too. She was at his mercy, after all, her body his instrument to play.

"You gotta let me come," she pleaded.

"No more chocolate cream-cheese muffins," he murmured before taking a mouthful of her breast. "Not while you're my submissive."

"Sure."

"Or anything that's a comparable substitute, like chocolate croissants, cheese danishes, or mocha-caramel-choco-chip freezes."

She groaned. "Okay, okay. Fucking task-master."

He squeezed her boob before pulling out the metal clamps. She couldn't help but be a little frightened by the clamps. They looked much bigger than she would have expected. She braced herself as he attached a clamp to the topside of one nipple. It wasn't the tip of the nipple, so it didn't hurt as bad as she'd thought.

"Hold this," he instructed, presenting the chain to her lips.

She took it between her teeth. He affixed the other clamp to the other nipple. Now it was fucking uncomfortable because her nipples were tugged upward by the chain in her mouth. Fitting his body close to hers, he put his hands on her waist. One hand slid up her back, caressing, cupping her neck. His other hand pulled the side of her thong down past a hipbone and wedged his fingers at her mound, stroking her. The ache in her nipples added an urgency to the pleasure he was amping. She wanted to come, she needed to come. She wanted and needed relief for her nipples and her pussy.

"Please, may I come, Sir?" she mumbled through the chain.

"Promise to be good," he murmured beside her ear.

"I promise to be good. Sir."

He stepped away from her and she suppressed a whimper at the loss of contact. His closeness, his heat, both aggravated and satiated her burning desire. She watched as he took off his undershirt.

Yeah, baby. Now they were getting somewhere. If she didn't have to hold onto the chain, she would have licked her lips at his nice set of pecs.

He dropped his pants next, revealing boxer briefs. Very, very sexy. But the best part was the bulge in the center. She wanted to rub it, grind her body against it.

"Very, very good, Sir," she added.

With a half-smile, he approached her and stood with his chest and his pelvis half an inch from hers. Leaning down, he brushed his lips on the side of her neck. He kissed his way down to her collarbone. She breathed in a satisfied sigh and arched herself into him. He wrapped an arm around her waist and pressed her even closer. His erection dug into her pelvic bone. He was hard, deliciously hard. She wrapped an arm around his hip in an attempt to angle her pussy onto his crotch. His free hand gripped her elevated thigh, molding her body to his. She could see parts of herself in the mirror—her bare leg draped over his hip and across his sculpted ass, the chain trapped between her lips. She saw the muscles of his back, his legs. The sight of their hot bodies entwined together enflamed her lust. As he started to work his mouth up the other side of her neck, she ground herself at him, wishing his lips could kiss every inch of her body all at once, though she would be more than satisfied to touch every inch of her to an inch of him.

"I want you to want me bad," he murmured below her ear.

She arched herself as much as the bonds permitted. "I do, Sir, I do."

At the moment, there was nothing more she wanted than to be fucked by him. She would have told him as much, but it was too much to say with her teeth clenched around a chain.

He threaded a hand through her hair and pulled so that she looked up at him. His eyes were like a pool of gems.

"Do you?" he asked.

"You expecting me to beg?" she responded, though most of the words came out garbled.

"Did you just say you were going to beg?" he teased.

She grunted.

"Begging is good."

She stared at him. "Just fuck me."

"Sir."

"Sir."

He pulled out his shaft. *Hallelujah!* Reaching for both her legs, he hoisted them over his hips. He wasn't going to bother with their underwear? she wondered for a second before deciding she couldn't wait either. Her pussy burned for something to fill it.

The tip of his hardness pressed between her legs. He fit his mouth over hers. "What was it you wanted?"

"Fuck me."

"Love a woman who knows what she wants."

With that he pressed himself into her, sliding the crown past the fabric of her thong, which had been brushed aside earlier from his fondling. She groaned.

God, it felt so good to have something inside her at last! She did her best to angle herself to receive more of him. He obliged and sank his cock further into her moist heat.

"Fuck," he exhaled when she clasped his shaft. "You must do your Kegel exercises."

She smiled to herself. Yep, she did.

Slowly, he began to move in and out of her. It felt marvelous. Amazing. Her body was already coiled, ready for release that anything hard and cylindrical would have satisfied, but with the way he moved, touching the most sensitive parts of her, filling her, it was the most glorious thing she could have experienced. Her pussy took him in greedily, hungrily, but since he held her by the legs, he dictated the motions and the pace.

"Don't come yet," he warned when she felt herself climbing the peak.

How long was he going to make her wait? Not too much longer, right? She wanted it so bad, needed it so bad. She wasn't sure she could hold it back. She was trying, but...*God, he felt too good.*

She whimpered as he rolled his hips more forcefully at her, knocking her back into the bedpost. He loosened his grip on her legs, allowing her to use her thigh muscles to move herself up and down his erection. He would meet her descent with a swift thrust, making her boobs bounce and the clamps to pull on her nipples, but any pain she felt was overshadowed by her desperate need to come. She was now balanced on the apex, wanting to fall over the other side.

"Please," she murmured, slowing down her motions. Hell, maybe she should just go for it. He couldn't stop her from coming, right?

"Please, what?" he demanded, shoving himself deep inside of her.

She moaned. "Sir. Please, sir."

"Good girl. You may come."

She wasn't even sure she had heard him because her climax was an explosion that wiped out everything, even the pinching of her nipples as he battered himself into her. If he didn't have such a secure hold of her and if she weren't tied to the bedpost, she would have fallen to the floor, a wreck of nerves and spasms, her limbs jerking uncontrollably as her orgasm erupted into every pore of her body. He thrust into her rapidly and found his own release. When the last of his cum had mixed with her wetness, she was still trembling. He set her legs back down, untied the rope, and swept her into the bed before she collapsed onto the floor. He took the chain from her mouth and unclasped the nipple clamps. She lay listening to the beating of her own heart. Her pussy still throbbed. Shudders still went through her legs.

Holy shit.

She was in trouble.

17

Really?" Audrey responded as she watched her boss gather the files off his desk and place them into his briefcase.

"Roy said he enjoyed working with you," Carl said. "Thought you could be a real asset on a new client they acquired."

Audrey mulled it over. Yet another opportunity on the East Coast.

"One of the Managing Directors in the DC office, Shawna Williams, had to take an unexpected leave because of her daughter's terrible car accident."

"I heard about it."

"Honestly, Shawna's going to be out for a long time. Which means the company's going to need an interim. I still think you have a great shot at a promotion in Fort Lauderdale. But, who knows, you might get your choice of Fort Lauderdale or DC."

Audrey took in a deep breath and let it out slowly.

Carl smiled at her. "I wish the opportunity were in this office. I'd hate to lose you."

"I appreciate you putting in a good word for me."

"I didn't need to do much. Your work speaks for itself. I think they'd want you in DC next month. I can have Drew step in for you here. Anyway, you think it over. Let me know by the end of the week."

"Okay, thanks, Carl."

He put on his coat and wished her good night. She stood looking out the window at the city skyline. It was past seven at night and many of the lights in the office buildings around them were off, and the fog had settled in. She wondered what the skyline of DC would look like. In many ways, she thought she'd be more at home in DC than Fort Lauderdale. She wasn't much of a beach person—hadn't even been to the coast in San Francisco till Rance—and the metropolitan quality, the universities, the museums, and the energy of being in the country's political power center appealed to her.

And Roy was in DC. Of course she wouldn't make her decision based on him, but it didn't hurt either.

And as soon as she thought of Roy, she thought of Rance. If she left San Francisco, there was no chance of their getting back together. But why was that even a consideration? It wasn't as if they had a chance of getting back together even if she stayed. Frustrated with herself, she went back to her office to lose the strange line of her thinking in work. At her computer, she pulled up the cash flow program her analyst had put together. Something hadn't been quite right with the numbers. She should leave it to the junior analyst to figure out what was wrong, but the young man had seemed stuck and so she had offered to take a look at it. She stared at the spreadsheet and examined the first set of formulas, but her mind wandered back to Rance.

Did she want to get back together with him? Did he want to get back together with her? She fingered the black pearl earrings. She had decided it was silly not to wear them. It wouldn't do any good for the pair to sit in the box, and she didn't feel quite right about giving them away. Was Charlene's assessment about the earrings right? Did it mean Rance hadn't given up on the idea of their getting back together?

She forced her mind back to DC. She was sure if she went to DC and impressed Roy enough, a Managing Director position was hers. Roy had been with the company a long time and was known to be really close to the CEO. Even if there was a slight, really remote, chance of her and Rance getting together, why would she pass up the opportunity? It was why they broke up in the first place. Wasn't it? Strange how the particulars seemed to be fading with time.

She stared at the computer screen and half-heartedly reviewed the inputs. She was about to examine the vectors when a knock at her door made her jump. She had thought she was the last person in the office. Looking up, her heart stalled.

It was Rance.

"*Bonsoir*," he greeted, looking unfairly debonair even though his hair was a little damp and tussled and he was dressed casually in faded jeans, a simple pull-over shirt and jacket. Actually, the man always looked good in jeans. It helped that he had long lean legs.

Unlike her own. Try as she might, she couldn't trim the fat from her thighs. And though she knew it shouldn't matter that she wasn't as hot as him, she couldn't help but believe people saw the imbalance.

"*B-Bonsoir*," she replied, unsure why her heart fluttered. "You had business in the building?"

"Passing through." He held up a paper bag. "Chinese? It's Tin's."

She smiled. It was their favorite hole-in-the-wall restaurant just outside of Chinatown. It was where Chinese people ate. No ambience, no frills, but killer food.

"I guess we better unpack it," she said, gesturing to the corner of the paper bag that was sodden with sauce.

It dripped onto his shoe. "*Merde.* I miss plastic bags."

Getting up from her desk, she found some paper towels for him as he set the take-out on the coffee table beside him.

"Well, they are bad for the environment. Except I have the kind you can reuse and carry with you in your purse 'cause it folds into this tube no bigger than a tampon."

Rance grinned. "If only I carried a purse."

"Just passing through, huh?" she asked after unpacking green beans in oyster sauce, empress prawns, peppered fish, and rice.

He wiped his shoe. "Where else would you be at this hour?"

She started at the implication.

"I did not mean that as—as anything negative."

"Like that I don't have a life?"

"You've always been hard-working."

"It's okay. I don't have a life."

An awkward silence ensued. As he sat down on the sofa, she handed him chopsticks and remembered that she had learned how to use chopsticks from him, a Frenchman. With his frequent meetings with Asian investors and travels to Asia, he had been quite adept at the utensil. She sat in a chair on the other side of the coffee table.

"They didn't pack you plates," she observed, getting up. "There should be some in the office kitchen."

"Don't need them unless you're worried about sharing germs. What would you like to start with?"

"The green beans."

Sitting back down, she accepted the container from him. She wondered how Stephanie would feel about their sharing food like they were family.

"You don't have a charity event or social function to attend?" she asked as a roundabout way of asking why he wasn't with Stephanie at the moment.

"I do, but I'm not attending."

"Oh."

He had come to see her. He had blown off other engagements to see her. She didn't know if she should be excited or not.

"I have to prepare for a trip anyway," he said, looking more at his prawns than at her.

"Yeah? Where you going?"

"Hong Kong."

"On pleasure or business?"

"Business."

She paused and attempted more nonchalance than she felt. "Stephanie get to go with you?"

He shook his head. They ate in silence for a while, which was nothing new for them. Rance used to comment that Americans ate too fast to enjoy their food. But the silence grew too often and too long toward the end of the relationship.

"Prawns?" he offered.

They exchanged containers.

"How is the wedding planning?" he asked.

"Good. Great. I think. Depends who you ask. Izzy is having the time of her life."

"And Jan isn't?"

"Jan would've been happy getting married by the Clerk-Recorder at City Hall. Lot less expensive."

"So they've come to a compromise."

"One more than the other, I think," she admitted. It had always been so easy to confide in Rance, but she was surprised that their time away hadn't changed that.

"Are you worried?"

"I shouldn't be. I mean, Jan and Izzy have been together for a long time. It's like they were made for each other."

"But you're worried."

And there was that, too. He could see into her so clearly, could speak her state of mind before she was aware of it herself. But he just didn't seem to get her when it came to the two of them.

"Jan seems more distressed than usual."

"Conflict is present in every relationship. It's how they get through it that matters."

"Jan said the right relationship fits like a glove."

"Bullshit."

His adamancy surprised her.

"Some relationships fall on difficult times, but they can emerge stronger for it," he explained.

Was he alluding to their own? Was this why he had come to see her, to talk about them? If so, how was she going to respond?

"How long you going to be in Hong Kong?" she asked to give herself time to think.

"A month. Maybe more." He put his container down and looked at her. "I have a confession to make."

Her heart accelerated faster than a race car. What in the world could he have to confess? That her Tahitian black pearl earrings were fake? But his look was far too serious for that.

"Uh, okay," she said, her mind going wild. He was coming out of the closet. She should've known a guy who looked so gorgeous in form-fitting jeans, with his education and sophistication, his lovemaking abilities, couldn't be straight.

"I was at Trey's Naughty Noel party."

Oh no. He had gotten it on with Charlene. Wait. Didn't Charlene say she hadn't hooked up with anyone at that event?

"And at the New Year's Eve of Erotica," he added.

She blinked.

"Soy Zorro."

Her eyes widened, and it was hard to breathe. He looked a little worried.

"You…you were Zorro?" she managed to get out.

"*Sí. Ouí.* I mean, yes."

She stared at the coffee table, trying to process the bombshell. She looked back up at him. "And the—the guy on the balcony at the Naughty Noel?"

He nodded.

Holy shit. Her office felt confining. She got to her feet to give herself space.

"The Naughty Noel was supposed to be a solitary event—a one-time event," he said, also getting up. "But afterwards, I couldn't resist."

She put a hand to her temple. "So you knew all along but you led me to believe..."

"I'm sorry."

"Okay, impersonating an escort was one thing, but this—this is something else."

"It's a little messed up. I'm sorry."

"A little?"

She started pacing. "I don't get it. Was it a dare from Blaine?"

"Blaine only gave me the invitation."

"Why did you wait until now to tell me?"

"Would it have made a difference if I told you earlier?"

"Yes! You should've told me when—before we—" She gestured her hands then clasped them together.

"Am I that revolting?"

"Yes! No! I mean, I wouldn't have if I'd known."

He straightened, his frown obvious.

She stared at him, a part of her in disbelief, the other part of her angry and upset that this hoax had been perpetrated on her. She rubbed her temples. Her brain hurt.

"I think," she tried. "I think you should go."

"Audrey, I didn't—"

"Just...*go*."

He stared back at her, clearly upset as well. He pressed his lips into a firm line and grabbed his jacket off the sofa.

"I'm...I'm sorry," he said, shrugging into his jacket.

As quickly as he had appeared, he was gone. Shaking, she sat on the edge of her desk. Rance. All along it had been Rance. Maybe she should be relieved that it had been someone she knew and not some shady stranger. But how could Rance have done that to her? Kept her in the dark while he was having his fun? There was no way she would have gone through with it if she'd known it was him. No way. If he'd known who she was, and she hadn't been in costume at the Naughty Noel, then it was wrong of him not to have revealed himself.

Suddenly, she couldn't wait to get to DC.

Charlene felt her pussy clench about the gently vibrating egg inside her. She was bent over on her knees in the middle of Blaine's bed, her wrists pinioned together and pulled between her thighs, causing her boobs and the side of her face to press into the bed linen below.

"I'm gonna go crazy if you don't fuck me, Sir," she gasped.

Blaine was on his knees behind her. Both of them were completely naked. His cock was long and hard. And she needed him inside of her.

"I've been a good girl, Sir," she said.

He dragged his cock along her clit. "Yeah?"

She shivered, feeling her legs go weak. "Yeah. No m-mocha-caramel-choco-chip freezes. Nothing from the café downstairs. Just a bagel and cream cheese for breakfast."

"Lunch?"

He massaged one buttock while continuing to run his cock along her folds. She wished she could grab it somehow.

"Minestrone soup."

"Soup can be high in sodium, but it's an improvement."

"Afternoon snack?"

"A vegetable fruit smoothie with kale and apples."

"Wow. When you're good, you're good."

"So fuck me already! Sir."

Using the remote control, he increased the intensity of the vibrations. "You deserve this."

He rubbed his cock harder and faster against her. Within seconds, she came all over his shaft. He eased the vibrations back to low as she continued to tremble and shake.

"Oh, God," she moaned. "Thank you, Sir."

He grasped a buttock. "You were so good, I'm tempted to take your ass."

"P-Please do."

He spread her wetness over his shaft and pressed the tip of his erection into her back hole. "Such a fucking hot ass."

Her anus gripped him tight. It hurt so good. He turned the vibrations back up again. She felt her teeth begin to chatter in her head, and pleasure soon overtook the discomfort in her rectum. He turned the egg onto its maximum level, and she exploded, soaking the sheets below. He scooped up more of her juices and popped out of her ass to lubricate his cock more. With the egg still on its highest setting, he sank his cock back into her, deeper this time. Still recovering from the second orgasm and distracted by the vibrating egg, she didn't notice how far he had penetrated. When she did, the fullness was *amazing.* Her body couldn't be more stimulated. She was going out of her mind with the pleasure of it all. Slowly, he began a thrusting action. She dug her fingernails into the bed sheet, though it wasn't easy with her wrists tied together.

The sensation from her ass was so different, so acute, so overwhelming, so delightful. She groaned long and low when he plunged himself deep, his balls slapping against her. He grabbed her by the hips and varied his rhythm, sometimes gentle, sometimes hard. When he sensed her ascending toward her climax, his motions became more rhythmic.

"Yes! Yes!" she cried, enjoying the fact that she didn't have to do much, loving the way his cock lit up every nerve.

She came into her orgasm with a scream, imploding and exploding at the same time. Her limbs would've been flying all over the place if she hadn't been forced into her position. She wanted to collapse but held her ass up so that he could finish. He rammed his cock into her with several hard thrusts before she felt the heat of his seed soaking her bowels. He held her by the waist as his body jerked against her. With a final shudder, he eased himself from her. He flipped her onto her back just as her thighs were about to slide out from under her. Reaching for the remote, he turned off the egg and removed it, then fell onto the bed beside her, his breathing hard.

"Damn…" he swore. "Your ass is so amazing."

Her wrists still bound, she brushed the perspiration from her brow and ran her fingers into her hair. "I'm surprised we didn't do more of that."

"It took you a while to back down from all your junk food."

"Yeah? Well, I'd get headaches if I didn't get my mocha-caramel-choco-chip freezes." She turned onto her side to face him. "Though the quickie we had in your car yesterday helped."

"If we didn't have jobs, I'd come over and fuck you anytime you wanted."

Mmmmm. How nice it would be if every time she craved a mocha-caramel-choco-chip freeze, she could call Blaine to come over and satisfy her appetite instead. The week had passed so quickly. She couldn't believe that this was their last day. To her surprise, she had enjoyed every minute of it, both the punishments and the rewards. And it didn't hurt that he had put her on a healthier diet. Audrey had been impressed.

"Should've known sex was the motivator for you," Audrey had said.

But not just any sex, Charlene had thought to herself. It had to be knock-her-socks-off sex. And Blaine had delivered. His company wasn't bad neither. In fact, he was a fun guy to hang out with.

"Would you want to go to Jan and Izzy's wedding?" she blurted. "It's in two weeks. Saturday."

She had intended to go stag but the idea of going with Blaine appealed to her. Suddenly, she felt nervous. She had just ask Blaine out *on a date.*

"I'm in Tahoe that weekend. Had a ski trip planned with some buddies from biz school."

Getting up, he straddled her legs and untied the rope around her wrists.

"Too bad," she huffed nonchalantly, though deep down she was disappointed. "The reception's at the Montecito Hotel, it's a quaint little place and I got a room with a Jacuzzi. You around this weekend?"

"I'm in Seattle for a week, then I got to work with Rance to oversee his remodel. He's headed for Hong Kong in two weeks."

In other words, I'm busy, she rephrased for him. Well, no big deal. She had agreed to one week with him, nothing more. It was just about the sex. It had been fun. It wasn't like she was trying to date him or anything.

He tossed the rope aside. "Let's go shower, then I'll take you to that corner restaurant you liked so much."

"I'll take a shower," she replied, taking his hand and getting out of bed. "But since this is our last night together, don't you think we should fuck each other's brains out? Sir?"

He whistled. "Damn. You make a compelling argument."

She slid off the bed and cocked her head at him. "And I didn't go to no four-year college neither."

18

Audrey had a sinking feeling as she looked once more around the dressing room in the small non-denominational church where Izzy and Jan's wedding was to take place. The ceremony was scheduled to start in fifteen minutes. The bride and her family were using one of the meeting rooms as their dressing room, and the last time Audrey had checked, Izzy and her family were fully ready.

But Jan was nowhere to be found.

Audrey even checked the men's bathroom. No Jan. Looking outside the window, she saw a blue and cloudless sky. The weather couldn't have been better. Maybe Jan had gone outside for some fresh air. She hoped that was the case.

Picking up her skirts, she went outside and walked around the front and sides of the building. No Jan. Just one of the guests rushing up the front steps. Izzy had once joked that her family, being Latino, were never on time. Hopefully the ceremony wouldn't need to be delayed for other reasons.

The back of the church was a community garden. If Jan wasn't there, then Audrey didn't know where Jan could be. Pushing the gate open, Audrey entered the garden. She walked past planter boxes, a small cactus area, and was about to give up when she heard something stir. In the very back of the garden was a willow tree. Jan sat on a small marble bench in the tree's shadow. In her slim black dress suit, she looked smart.

"I've been looking all over for you," Audrey said. "We have, like, five minutes before the ceremony is supposed to start."

Jan stared at the ground. "I know."

She did not have the tone of someone excited about the most special day in her life. Audrey took a seat beside her and said nothing.

"I never thought I would get cold feet," Jan said after a spell of silence. "I mean, I knew Izzy was the one I wanted to be with since day one."

"Yeah, we all envied you two. You have something special between you."

"I even considered having kids because Izzy wants kids, and I'm not much of a kid person."

"You thinking differently now?"

"No, but…this whole wedding thing. We have different approaches to finance."

"You have different approaches to a lot of things."

Jan got up. "Yeah, but you hear that most failed marriages revolve around two things: sex and money.

We haven't even gotten married and we're on the wrong footing with money."

"Doesn't mean it can't be worked out."

"And if it can't? I don't want to have this wedding for nothing if we're broken up a few years down the line."

"Are you saying you don't want to be with Izzy?"

"I do! I'm crazy about her. I can't imagine living without her."

"Sounds like you should marry Izzy."

Sitting back down, Jan stared at the ground again. "But we should to be a perfect fit, like a glove. No wrinkles. Nada."

"Relationships aren't gloves. They have conflict. They fall on hard times. But if you make it through, you'll only be stronger."

Wait a minute, Audrey thought to herself. Those words sounded awfully familiar...like the ones Rance had spoken last week. With all the last-minute wedding work, she hadn't had a whole lot of time to reflect on his confession. She'd been grateful for the distraction of the wedding, but she couldn't shake off the bombshell he'd dropped. She had been tempted to talk with one of her girlfriends about it, but Izzy and Jan obviously had their hands full, and Charlene seemed to be having PMS--she was off her diet and back to ordering croissants and mocha-caramel-choco-chip-freezes but barely took more than a few bites or sips. It hadn't helped that she'd had a wet dream with "Zorro" a few nights ago.

There was no denying she was still very drawn to Rance sexually. He could rev her up and satisfy her like no one and nothing else. But just because they were physically compatible, even intellectually compatible, didn't mean they were emotionally compatible.

But maybe it wasn't about compatibility. The truth was she still loved him. When things were good between them, they were *really good.* There was simply a whole new level of fun, interest, and meaning in life with him. Maybe she had been too hasty in letting the times when things weren't going well outweigh all that was positive. Like she had just told Jan, there will be conflict, there will be turmoil. It's how a couple weathered those storms that mattered. In the end, those storms didn't have to rule the day.

"What more could you guys ask for?" Audrey added to Jan. "Of course you're not going to see eye to eye on everything, but you have trust, love, friendship, commitment. If those aren't ingredients to a winning combination, then I don't know what is."

Jan turned to Audrey. "You really believe that?"

"I do," she replied softly.

"But..." Jan hesitated. "Other couples have had those ingredients, too."

"You mean like me and Rance?"

Jan bit her bottom lip and nodded.

"Maybe we didn't try hard enough. Or maybe I didn't try hard enough. Maybe I made a mistake in letting him go."

"Really?"

"Maybe. This step you and Izzy are taking, especially given that you didn't even have the right to get married not too long ago, it's special. It's inspiring. It's your day,

I'm glad to be part of it, but damn if I don't get your happily-ever-after for myself."

They exchanged smiles. Audrey put her arm around Jan and gave her a big squeeze.

"Come on," Audrey coaxed, "we're gonna be late for your wedding and I thought Asians were always on time."

"That's a stereotype. Just because we have superior math skills doesn't mean we're timely," Jan joked.

"Now who's being a stereotype?"

They got up, arm in arm, and headed back inside the church.

"How come you're not out on the dance floor?"

From her table, Charlene watched the happily married couple get on the dance floor to Kate Perry's *I Kissed A Girl*. The reception was held in a small boutique hotel, and it was the perfect size for the sixty or so guests. She, Audrey, and Izzy's family had worked most of the day before decorating the room. They had done such a good job making the most of their limited budget that she was inspired to consider being a wedding planner. Something more creative than working at Stevenson & Young.

"Maybe later," she told Audrey as she swirled her maraschino cherry around her martini glass.

"I guess there aren't exactly a lot of straight guys here," Audrey said as she took a seat next to her.

"Yeah, I hit on that sexy brother over there, but he's gay."

"Well, that hasn't stopped you from dancing before."

After finishing her cherry, Charlene took a sip of her martini.

"You're not moping over Blaine are you?" Audrey asked.

"What?" she replied, offended. "When have I ever moped over a guy? There's plenty of fish in the sea, even in the gayest city in America."

"He hasn't called since the end of your, uh, thing?"

Charlene shrugged. "He's been busy. And our *thing* is done with. I'm not expecting or waiting around for a call or text or email or anything from him. I hate all that awkward shit. Izzy and Jan are totally lucky, though, they never went through stuff like that. Their relationship was always smooth sailing."

Audrey was silent. "Well, remember when Izzy hadn't come out to her family yet? Jan was pretty upset about that. We don't ever have to go through anything like that."

"True that. My parents just want me to marry some nice young black man, preferably with a college degree."

"So a white guy would never fit the bill for them."

"My folks are more old-fashioned than yours. Your parents liked Rance, right?"

"Yeah, though if they knew some of the things he'd done...you know he was the mystery guy at Trey's Naughty Noel and the Eve of Erotica?"

"He told you?"

"Last week. Just dropped by my office, said he had a confession to make and...wait a minute. You knew. You knew it was him!"

Charlene hastily swallowed the last of her martini. "What?"

"You knew! You didn't look shocked at all when I told you just now."

"I was! I just didn't—oh, hell. Okay, I knew."

"And you didn't tell me?"

"It was Blaine's fault! He told me after the Christmas party, then wanted me to get you to the Eve of Erotica."

Audrey folded her arms. "And?"

"'Cause Rance wanted to see you again. I didn't know anything else. My job was just to convince you to go the party. Guess you know the rest."

She waited for Audrey's reaction, hoping her friend wasn't mad at her.

A server came by. "Cake?"

"I can't believe you didn't tell me," Audrey said after two slices of *dulce de leche* had been left with them.

"I figured it wasn't up to me. It was Rance's thing."

Audrey pursed her lips and stared at the cake in front of her. "Why didn't he just tell me he wanted to see me?"

"Hell if I know. Guess the guy has a kinky streak. And maybe he's a little intimidated by you. People always intimated by strong black women."

The thought seemed to amuse Audrey.

"So what did you say after he confessed?" Charlene asked, relieved Audrey wasn't furious, as she put her fork into the cake.

"I was mad. I made him leave."

"Whaddya do that for?"

"What you mean what'd I do that for? You wouldn't have been upset? He knew all along who I was."

"I'd have been flattered. Turned on. Hell, it's his shoes I wouldn't have wanted to be in. Imagine seeing your girl getting off on some mystery guy that she thinks isn't you."

"But I'm not his girl."

"You still have the hots for him. You still love him. And apparently, he still has it in for you."

Audrey took in a deep breath and let it out slowly. "Shit. I messed up. Again."

"No big deal. Just call him up. Get him a belated Christmas gift."

"I think he's in Hong Kong."

"I'm pretty sure Blaine said he leaves this weekend. He might still be here."

Audrey perked up. Charlene was already fishing in her purse for her cell.

"I could call and ask Blaine."

"Rance is staying at the *sur Mer*. Try the hotel first."

Charlene couldn't help but be a little disappointed at not being able to use her excuse for calling Blaine, but she looked up the number for the *Hotel sur Mer*. She handed the phone to Audrey.

"Hi, uh, is, uh, the owner, I mean, is, uh," Audrey stuttered into the phone.

Charlene took the phone from her. "Is Mr. Durand there?"

"I believe so," the receptionist replied. "Whom may I ask is calling?"

"He hasn't left for Hong Kong then."

"He leaves tonight. His cab arrives in less than an hour. Do you want me to put you through to his room?"

"Yes, please." Charlene handed the phone over to Audrey, who looked scared shitless. "He leaves for the airport in an hour."

Audrey took the phone tentatively.

"Go on, girl," Charlene encouraged. "It's a sign. Fate. You caught him just in time."

"I don't know about this. It's awkward over the phone. I should wait till he gets back from Hong Kong."

"He's there for a while, according to Blaine. That's why Blaine's so busy. He's overseeing the remodel of the hotel's restaurant for Rance."

"It's just ringing. He's not there," Audrey said with relief.

Charlene scowled. "We'll try again."

"No, I don't even know what to say. This kind of thing has to be done in person. So you can read their expression and have a better idea what they're thinking."

Charlene took her phone back and looked at the clock. "Then go over there."

"What?"

"*Go over there.* It'll probably take you forty minutes to get to the *sur Mer*. That's before his cab arrives."

"What?"

"Catch him before he leaves for Hong Kong!"

Charlene felt a rush of adrenaline at her own idea.

"I can't leave now! Hello? We're at Jan and Izzy's wedding reception."

"The important stuff is over. There's just dancing now. Go. Get."

"I'm one of the bridesmaids!"

Charlene grabbed Audrey by the arm and dragged her onto the dance floor where Jan and Izzy had just finished smooching to cheers of the guests around them.

"Audrey has less than an hour to get to Rance and spill her guts about how she still loves him before he leaves for Hong Kong forever," Charlene informed them.

Audrey narrowed her eyes. "He's not going to be there—"

"Who knows how long he's going to be in Hong Kong. This could be her last chance."

Izzy shrieked. "You *do* still love him!"

"I guess so," Audrey mumbled, looking away from all the onlookers.

Izzy threw her arms around Audrey. "I'm so happy for you!"

"But she has to go *now*," Charlene said. "A cab's arriving to take him to the airport any minute."

"Yes! Go, *amiga*, go to the love of your life! This is definitely the best day of my life! Go! *Rapidamente!*"

"I can't leave your reception—" Audrey protested.

"If you meant what you told me," Jan said to her with a serious stare, "don't you think you should go?"

"But I was going to—"

"Go. There's nothing we or one of our family members can't handle."

"Go!" Izzy cried.

"Okay, okay," Audrey relented.

The three of them practically shoved Audrey out the room.

"I'm not even dressed!" she said in a last attempt at balking.

"Stop being such a wuss!" Charlene scolded. "You want some exotic Asian chick to get her hands on Rance before you do?"

"Right. I'm going."

Jan had grabbed Audrey's purse and handed it to her. They watched her hustle from the hotel.

"I get the feeling we're gonna have another wedding in the not-so-distant future!" Izzy said, giving Jan a gleeful hug.

"We'll see," Jan answered.

"I don't think Rance is going to let her get away a second time," Charlene said with a stab of wistfulness. She turned to Jan and Izzy. "Now, you think I can get one of these hunky queers to try pitching for the other team?"

"Don't be a wuss," Audrey echoed to herself as she climbed into her small Toyota Corolla. With her voluminous skirts, she felt like she filled the whole car.

Heart racing, she drove the car out of the hotel garage and onto the street. Her cell phone dinged. She saw a text from Charlene:

Just tried Rance's room again. Maybe he's in the bar?

There were a lot of places in the hotel he could be. He could be in the lobby, his office, a meeting room. This was crazy, trying to catch him before he left for the airport. He wouldn't have the time to talk. He probably wouldn't be in the mood to talk. What if he wasn't too happy with how she had received his "confession."

That was all self-doubt talk. Like Jan, she was getting cold feet. But Jan had faced her fears. It was *her* turn now.

Driving through the evening traffic, she was so nervous she couldn't think of what she would say to Rance if she did catch him. *I can't believe I'm doing this.* She turned her car onto the Great Highway. When the majestic *Hotel sur Mer* came into view, her heart was pounding like it wanted to exit her chest. This was where it had all started after their initial meeting in Yerba Buena Gardens. Rance had convinced her to spend the night with him at the hotel. She'd had no clue that he owned the friggin' place. To her, it would always be the most beautiful hotel, vintage, like something from the turn of the century.

A knock on the car window startled her from her reverie. It was the valet.

"Checking in, ma'am?" the young man asked.

"Uh, just stopping by," she replied.

She allowed him to open the door for her and stepped out. If he was shocked by her formal attire, he didn't show it. Leaving him with the car and keys, she walked into the lobby. With its beautiful rugs over shiny tiled floors, it was as gorgeous as she remembered. Gathering her nerves, she walked over the reception counter.

"Welcome to the *Hotel sur Mer*," greeted the receptionist—Stacey, according to the nametag.

"Hi, I'm looking for Rance," Audrey said.

"Oh, were you the one who called earlier?" the young woman asked. "I have a note about someone who was trying to reach Mr. Durand."

Stacey was friendly, as all the staff were, having been trained extensively in hospitality, but Audrey noticed the quick raise of the woman's eyebrows at her attire.

"No," Audrey replied. "I mean yes. Well, sort of. Is he here? I was hoping to catch him before he left for the airport."

"I'm not sure. I just started my shift. Do you want me to try his room?"

"No, we tried. I tried."

"Maybe if you have a seat, I can try to track him down for you."

"No, that's okay. It's not that important."

She was too restless to sit around a lobby. Plus, she didn't want to get stared at wearing a dress that appealed mostly to princess wannabes aged five and younger.

"I'll just, uh, take a quick look in the bistro bar," Audrey said.

But a peek in the bistro yielded nothing. She didn't want to go back to the receptionist and have to explain why she was trying to track down Rance while wearing a bridesmaid's dress. Even though it seemed Rance had checked out of his room, she decided to try it one more time. She took the elevator to the top floor. There were only two suites on that level, and she was pretty sure Rance was staying in one of them. She tried the suite that she and Rance used to occupy.

An elderly foreign woman answered the door.

"Are you room service?" she asked with a heavy middle-eastern accent as she surveyed Audrey's gown with puzzlement.

"I'm sorry, I must have the wrong room," Audrey said. "Mr. Durand is in the other suite."

"Ah, yes, the hotel owner. I believe he left." She turned her head and spoke to someone else in the room, then said to Audrey, "Yes, he left. My husband, he saw the suitcases."

"Thank you."

Audrey let out a big sigh after the woman had closed the door. Mindlessly, she walked across the foyer to the other suite and leaned against the wall. If only she had acted sooner. It wasn't as if all was lost. She simply had to email him. Maybe his cell number was still the same in Hong Kong. His hotel would know how to get ahold of him. And Blaine would.

But it wouldn't be the same trying to explain things long distance.

As if it would've made all the difference even if she had caught him before he left for the airport, she reasoned to herself.

She pressed her forehead to the wall. She shouldn't have gotten so angry at him over the whole Naughty Noel/Eve of Erotica charade. Charlene was just as guilty of the cover-up, but she wasn't about to forsake her friendship over it. A good part of her anger had been embarrassment that she had been caught red-handed getting off on some total stranger. What must he think of her? She had thought maybe he was just trying to prove something, that she still melted at his sexual abilities. But that really wasn't Rance's character. She knew him better than that.

"Audrey."

She stared at the wall in front of her, not sure if she was hearing things 'cause it sure as hell sounded like Rance's voice. For a moment, it seemed the world had stopped, except for the beating of her heart. Slowly, she turned her head to see him standing a few feet away. Realizing her forehead was still pressed to the wall, she straightened.

"Rance," she managed to voice. "I thought you left for the airport?"

"Stacey found me in my office," he replied, his stare serious. "Told me a woman wearing a prom dress was looking for me."

Audrey glanced down at her lavender satin. "Oh, I, uh, was at, you know, Izzy and Jan's wedding."

He said nothing.

She tried to lighten the mood between them. "I'm a little old for prom."

But his demeanor remained unchanged.

Exhaling a deep sigh, she decided to plunge in. "Charlene mentioned that you were headed to Hong Kong tonight. Guess Blaine told her. And I was thinking I owed you an apology for my reaction. And I wanted to do it in person if I could because, well, it just feels better that way."

Except maybe it wasn't given how stoic he looked. She would have done better on the phone not having to look into his intense stare.

Unnerved, she started to babble a little. "I got to thinking about...well, I'm not sure why I got so angry...maybe, it's because—I hope you didn't get too upset that I was angry. I'm not excusing my reaction, but you might see how it could be understandable, right?"

She took another deep breath. Why didn't he say something? Was he upset with her? Was he deliberately making this hard on her because she had been angry with him?

"But the truth is, when I was talking to Jan right before the wedding, because Jan was getting cold feet and wasn't sure she was gonna go through with it all—"

Even as she spoke, she was aware that she confided everything to Rance. All the crazy charades aside, she trusted with him anything and everything.

"I found myself telling her things that you had told me about how it's normal for relationships to have their rocky moments and that we—people—couples—can emerge stronger for them. And I just...I feel—I believe—"

Before she could finish her sentence, he had crossed the distance between them, cupped her face, and kissed her, a slow, deep, devouring kiss. Her pulse shot up into the stratosphere. She trembled with relief but returned his kiss as best as she could. It felt so good to have his lips on hers, so good to be so close to him again after all this time, in the light of day, not the darkness or behind a mask. This felt so right. He felt so right. When at last he came up for air, she was breathless, sure that her emotions were shining in her eyes. They looked at each in lengthy silence.

"I suppose I should let you catch your cab," she whispered.

He was still holding her, all the prior stoicism gone, replaced with obvious affection, with love. And she could not have felt more thrilled. He let her go, and she nearly protested the loss of his touch. Maybe he would let her ride in the cab with him so that they could talk. She watched him as he pulled out his cardkey from his wallet, reached around her, and unlocked the door. He swept her into the room by the waist, pulling her to his hip.

"Uh, what time's your flight?" she asked, her heart pounding at the prospect that he was going to try to squeeze in a quickie.

"Twelve-thirty," he replied.

She glanced at a clock in the foyer. "Your cab must be waiting for you. You got to go through customs and..."

Why was she telling him this when he was a hundred times more well-traveled than shc?

Still holding her, he picked up the phone with his free hand. "Stacey, cancel the cab…I'll take another flight to Hong Kong."

Her legs grew weak. They were going to do it. They hadn't done it since…since too long. Need and desire bowled into her. Paying for a new flight wasn't a big deal for Rance. He could afford it, so she shouldn't feel at all guilty that she had made him miss his original flight.

Nevertheless, she whispered, "Are you sure?"

He didn't answer. Instead, his mouth took hers. She wasn't sure if she was going to melt or go up in flames.

Or both, somehow. Because that's what it felt like. That's what his kisses did to her. He caressed, tasted, savored her mouth in a long, scintillating, probing kiss that made her head spin. She threw her arms around him and returned the pressure of his lips. She wanted to pour all her passion into the kiss. His arm snaked around her back, pressing her into him. She fit her body to his as close as she could while wearing a hundred layers of skirt.

His hands moved to cup her face next, tilting her chin so that he could clamp his mouth down on hers. His tongue delved into hers. She was content to let him guide the dance between their tongues till, burning with need, she parried with her own thrusts. Heat churned in her loins, making the dress suffocatingly hot. He was never going to be able to get her out of the darn thing. Well, if he couldn't get her undressed, at least one of them could be naked. She kissed her way down his throat and began unbuttoning his shirt. He took off his jacket, but before she could undo the last few buttons, he had reclaimed her mouth. As if he had not gotten enough, he kissed her long and deep. His hands caressed the nape of her neck and her back.

Abruptly, he turned her around and unzipped the dress. He pushed the gown and crinoline down in one easy movement as he went to one knee. It was as if he had undressed a thousand bridesmaids wearing poofy dresses before. When he turned her back around, she wished she had worn sexier lingerie. She had on her backless bra, which almost went down to her waist, a simple pair of satin bikini briefs and thigh-high stockings. But it didn't matter. Seeing the fire in his eyes made her feel sexy as hell. His gaze devoured her.

Grasping her hips, he pressed his mouth to the space of bare flesh between her backless bra and her panties. He tongued her belly button, and her legs quivered. He ran his hands up her sides as he stood, taking her arms with him and pinning them above her head to the wall behind her. Holding her there, he took mouthfuls of her neck, his lips brushing the soft spot beneath her jaw. She took in a breath to cool herself. She was so turned on, a quickie would have been just fine with her. When he pressed his hips into her, she groaned with need. Memories of Trey's Naughty Noel and the New Year's Eve of Erotica danced in her head.

Rance. It had been Rance all along. He had wanted her. Desired her still. And it was the most arousing thing in the world.

She ground her hips a little at him and he groaned. He released her wrists, undid the clasp of her bra and assailed the breasts he had just freed. He captured a nipple, sucked it gently, swirled his tongue around it, flicked it, then sucked it again. She could feel the sensation in two places: on her nipple and between her legs. She ran her fingers through his hair. She had always loved the way it felt, its slick softness. He massaged her other breast as he sucked on the nipple till she panted and writhed.

"Oh, Lord," she breathed.

He unclipped her garters, then went back to his knees. He shimmied her panties down. She stepped out of her heels. He spread her legs and then he was between them, his head buried at her mound, his tongue teasing her clit. She moaned at the exquisiteness rippling from that sensitive little bud. He always seemed to find just the right spot, too. Pleasure waved over her with each deliberate lick. *Damn. His tongue felt so damn good.*

Tension began to coil in her belly as she felt her climax approaching. She ran her hands over herself, gripping, grasping, as if doing so could diffuse the pressure that she both desired and dreaded. But as his tongue worked its magic strokes, she surrendered herself to the impending glory. It erupted inside of her, making her body shake. She slammed a hand against the wall as delight simultaneously radiated and imploded. As always, Rance pushed her to the edge, but guided her back down instead of leaving her to hang over the cliff she had just gone over. But before she could recover completely, he swept her into his arms and carried her to the nearest sofa.

He kissed her all over while she basked in the afterglow of her orgasm. Then his hand was between her thighs, stroking a new wave of desire to life. She was hot and wet . Reaching for his pants, she caressed the hardness at his crotch. Impatience surged in her. She unzipped his jeans. He shed them and pulled off his shirt. She ran her hands over the planes and ridges of his chiseled chest. He had a perfect body, and she might always feel a little self-conscious at the disparity between his body and hers. But she wasn't going to let it stand in the way this time.

"Look at me, Audrey."

She pulled her gaze away from his pecs and met his smoldering stare.

"Je t'aimerai toujours."

She wasn't entirely sure what he had said. I will love you always?

Before she could inquire, however, his mouth claimed hers once more. She wrapped her arms around him and pulled him close. She angled her hips. Taking the invitation, he sank himself into her. As wonderful as her previous climax had been, this was even better. To be filled by him, to feel him inside of her.

"*Mon dieu*," he breathed.

With a smile, she began grinding herself at him. He met her with his own thrusts. In the darkness of the room lit only from the moon and stars outside, they made love, their bodies undulating in rapturous rhythm. Pleasure rippled to the tips of her toes. She quickened her motions. He deepened his thrusts. Another orgasm loomed large and beautiful. But she wanted to make sure he came, too, and so she flexed her vaginal muscles around his hardness. He murmured something unintelligible in French, then rolled his hips at her more forcefully. Her clasp tightened on him as her climax neared, closer and closer. When it finally crashed into her, her body went into spasms of ecstasy. Her eyes rolled to the back of her head, and her toes curled form the all-consuming intensity. Rance bucked against her, grunted, then fell into his own euphoric paroxysm.

"When is the next flight to Hong Kong?" she asked after she had recovered her breath and he had pulled from her.

"It doesn't matter."

"Doesn't matter?" she echoed.

He touched his forehead to hers and said in a husky tone, "I should never have let you get away. We will find a way to make this work. Okay?"

She nodded. There wasn't much more to say except, "*Ouí, ouí.*"

19

The hallway of the hotel wobbled before Charlene. Champagne always had a way of going straight to her head, more so than hard liquor, even. She put a hand to the wall. Maybe it was those damn bubbles. She shouldn't have done that third toast to Audrey, who hadn't called or texted in the last two or so hours. Which meant that she must have gotten ahold of Rance in time, and if she did, then there had to be a happy ending. Charlene smiled to herself. It had all been worth it. Even the fling with Blaine. She hadn't come away empty-handed. A year's worth of dining at Ballander's was better than any man she could have had at the moment. And though she hadn't been able to convert one of the gay men at the wedding or find an unattached straight guy, she couldn't complain. Izzy and Jan were happily married. Rance and Audrey would be happily married one day. All in all, it was a good day.

She fumbled with her keycard but managed to stumble into her room. Too bad the hotel didn't have a spa facility. Maybe she'd call Audrey in the morning and see if she could get checked into the *Hotel sur Mer* for a day. That girl sure had lucked out, falling in love with the owner of a posh hotel. Audrey was spending the night in a penthouse suite instead of being in one of these small rooms with the oddly placed light switch. Maybe she should open the door to let the hallway light in till she figured where the light switch was.

"I had trouble finding it, too."

A lamp in the sitting area came on. She blinked several times, then narrowed her eyes. Was it really Blaine sitting there on the sofa?

"It helps when you're not drunk," he said with a broad grin.

"Fuck you. How'd you get in here?" she demanded, setting her purse on the nearest table. It fell to the floor.

"I have my ways."

"That's—that's messed up. Last time I stay in this hotel if they be letting potential rapists into any goddamn room."

"Yeah, I had the same thought. You wear that to the wedding?"

She looked down at her burgundy-colored knit sheath and gold lace-up sandals. "What?"

"You're not supposed to show up the bride, looking that sexy."

"Aren't you supposed to be in Tahoe?"

"I was. Drove up at five in the morning so I could get in my black diamond runs."

Not being a skier, she didn't know what the hell black diamonds were and what gemstones had to do with mountains and skiing.

"So why're you here sittin' in the dark like some creepy pervert?"

"Waiting for you."

He got off the sofa, found a drinking glass, opened the fridge at the bar and retrieved a bottled water. He filled the glass and handed it to her.

"Waiting for me, huh?" she said, eying him dubiously before downing the water. Even in a simple long-sleeve cotton shirt, he looked pretty cute.

"Had a proposition for you. A very indecent proposal."

"Yeah, not interested."

She plopped down on an armchair beside the sofa he had occupied and tried to undo her sandals, but her fingers felt thick and the little buckles had shrunk in size since she had put them on. He knelt down in front of her and helped her with her shoes.

"Not even if I bribed you with a weekend in Yountville?" he asked. "Complete with dinner at The French Laundry?"

She considered it for a minute, but the champagne strengthened her forbearance. "Nope."

He slid the sandals from her feet and eyed her legs with obvious appreciation. He caressed the length of her calf.

"Hey, none of that," she said. "Or I'll call the cops on you."

He stared at her, the boyish grin replaced with a frown, but his hand continued to travel up her leg.

"I dare you to," he challenged.

She narrowed her eyes again. "Fuck you."

"You know I can make it worth your while. Don't tell me you don't want it."

His caress tickled the back of her knee and now her thigh. A familiar warmth was percolating in her loins already.

"Oh, sure, take advantage of a drunk girl."

She got to her feet and, walking to the bed, began to shimmy out of her dress. She had on a wine colored demi-corset with matching Brazilian cut panties. By the look in his eyes, she knew the lingerie had the impact it was meant to. Good. She wanted him to suffer.

"So you're not interested at all in my proposition?" he asked.

Turning her back—and ass—to him, she opened the nearby dresser. She had packed a babydoll nightie or she could opt for her tank top and flannel pajama pants. She opted for the babydoll. Just to make him squirm.

Holy shit, his expression read when she pulled out the nightie and threw it on the bed.

She tried to unhook the back of her corset. Again, he had to come to her aid.

"You don't even want to hear what it is?" he tried.

"Nope."

Surprised, he let the corset drop to the floor.

She turned to him and smiled. Patting him on the cheek, she said, "We had our fun, didn't we, white boy?"

In one quick movement, he had grabbed her wrist, pinned it behind her and shoved her onto the bed, his body pressing her down. His mouth was beside her ear.

"Now I told you not to call me 'white boy.'"

Her heart was racing, and that warm agitation below her waist was in full flare.

"Our week is up," she spat. "Now get the fuck off me."

"I would, but I don't think you really want me to."

What the fuck? He had some gall. She tried to push off the bed though she knew her effort would prove fruitless. She felt his hand at her hip. His other hand was still holding her wrist against her back.

"I bet," he said, "you're wet for me already. I bet I could get you to come real good."

The sultry tone of his voice made her shiver.

"That would be the champagne more 'an anything else," she mumbled.

He pulled one side of her panty past her hip bone and snaked his hand to her mound. "Would it? Then I guess, to prove my point, I better make love to you till you're sober."

She had expected him to say *fuck.* Instead, it sounded like he had said *make love.* Either way, the thought of getting it on all night with Blaine was more than titillating now. Two of his fingers grazed her clitoris. She moaned and knew there was no way she was going to win out if he was going to be like this.

"In fact, if I get you to come—while you're sober—I want you to be my submissive again."

Between the champagne and his fingers working their magic, she couldn't think straight. She better not agree to anything, even if it pleased the hell out of her that he wanted to be with her again. It was obvious he wanted her. Wanted her so bad he had driven to and from Tahoe in the same day. Which meant he was giving up at least another day of skiing.

"For how long?" she stalled.

"At least a week. Maybe a month. Maybe more."

He pressed his erection against her. She smiled to herself, ready now to give in to the desire flaming through her, ready to put herself in his very capable, very talented hands. He released his hold of her wrist and she rolled onto her back to face him. He kissed her all over from her neck to her breasts.

"I'll think about it," she murmured. "White boy."

He grunted and grabbed her buttock with a hard smack. She'd let him play the "master," but in the end, she was sure she wasn't the only one who would be doing all the submitting.

About the Author

After once accidentally flashing an audience with her knickers, Em Brown decided that writing was a safer pastime than theater. She writes both historical and contemporary erotic romance for readers to indulge their wicked desires--because everyone needs a little "me" time, a chance to unwind, lose themselves in a story, and, if they dare, get a little hot and bothered!

Em currently lives in the San Francisco Bay Area. A graduate of "nerd nation", she has gone from writing policy memos and government reports to writing naughty romances that she hopes will, for her female readers, at least, unleash the goddess within.

Connect with Em

www.facebook.com/embrownauthor
www.twitter.com/gddessunleashed

Join My Readers-Only Newsletter

Get a **FREE** sexy romance book from right now:
www.em-brown.com/freebook

OTHER WORKS BY EM BROWN

CAVERN OF PLEASURE SERIES

Mastering the Marchioness
Conquering the Countess
Binding the Baroness
Lord Barclay's Seduction

RED CHRYSANTHEMUM STORIES

(This series is available in individual parts, sets of five or the complete series)

Master vs. Mistress
Master vs. Mistress: The Challenge Continues
Seducing the Master
Taking the Temptress
Master vs. Temptress: The Final Submission
Wedding Night Submission
Punishing Miss Primrose, Parts I - XX

CHATEAU DEBAUCHERY SERIES

Submitting to the Rake
Submitting to Lord Rockwell
Submitting to His Lordship
Submitting to the Marquess
Submitting to the Baron

OTHER STORIES

Claiming a Pirate

Get Special Deals on More Best Selling Books

CPSIA information can be obtained
at www.ICGtesting.com
Printed in the USA
LVHW081521021219
639177LV00010B/375/P

9 781631 610264